Dramatic Pause

Also by P. G. Kain

THE SOCIAL EXPERIMENTS OF
DORIE DILTS
#1: *Dumped by Popular Demand*
#2: *The School for Cool*

COMMERCIAL BREAKS
#1: *Famous for Thirty Seconds*
#2: *Picture Perfect*

COMMERCIAL BREAKS

Dramatic Pause

BY P. G. KAIN

ALADDIN M!X

NEW YORK   LONDON   TORONTO   SYDNEY   NEW DELHI

ALADDIN M!X
Simon & Schuster Children's Publishing Division
1230 Avenue of the Americas, New York, NY 10020
First Aladdin M!X edition November 2012
Copyright © 2012 by P. G. Kain
All rights reserved, including the right of reproduction in whole or in
part in any form.
ALADDIN is a trademark of Simon & Schuster, Inc., and related logo
is a registered trademark of Simon & Schuster, Inc.
ALADDIN M!X and related logo are registered trademarks of
Simon & Schuster, Inc.
For information about special discounts for bulk purchases, please contact
Simon & Schuster Special Sales at 1-866-506-1949 or
business@simonandschuster.com.
The Simon & Schuster Speakers Bureau can bring authors to your live event.
For more information or to book an event contact the Simon & Schuster Speakers
Bureau at 1-866-248-3049 or visit our website at www.simonspeakers.com.
Designed by Jessica Handelman
The text of this book was set in Bembo.
Manufactured in the United States of America 1012 OFF
2 4 6 8 10 9 7 5 3 1
Library of Congress Control Number 2012948208
ISBN 978-1-4169-9788-7 (pbk)
ISBN 978-1-4169-9791-7 (eBook)

To my love, WBC,
for putting up with my dramatic paws

ACKNOWLEDGMENTS

I tend to dislike acknowledgments that thank every single person the author has ever met. That said, I would like to start by thanking the Phoenicians for developing the alphabet.

Moving on, I'd like to thank the many friends who support and encourage me in ways both seen and unseen. Thank you (in order of appearance), Beth (Sofia and Ruby), Rebekah, Shari, Sara, Justin, Pam, Carley, Chris, Loins, Olivia, Kate, Lyn, Greta, and Meline. Thanks to my family, Judi and Matt, for much love and support.

Thanks to my middle-grade pals, Julia DeVillers and Barbara Dee for perspective and camaraderie. To my middle-grade-book BFF, Taylor Morris, thank you for your amazing feedback on this manuscript, limitless generosity, and endless capacity to listen to me complain.

To William, thank you for being a friend. You are golden.

Thanks to my wonderful agent, Alyssa Eisner

Henkin, for her wisdom and winsome. Thanks to everyone at Simon & Schuster/Aladdin who worked on these books, including Jessica Sonkin Handelman, Carolyn Swerdloff, Lydia Finn, Annie Berger, Alyson Heller, and Liesa Abrams. Thanks to my editor, Fiona Simpson, for her enthusiastic and kind support from start to finish, and to Kate Angelella for getting things started.

I would never write an acknowledgement without thanking the most important person involved: YOU, the reader. Thanks for reading this book. If you've read this book, then you have finished the whole series and I appreciate that. I love to hear from readers, and I respond to every e-mail I get. Please visit me at www.TweenInk.com to find out about my next project, or send me an e-mail at pg@tweenink.com.

CHAPTER 1

"Nicole didn't do it. I did it!"

I can feel the space vibrating from the intensity in my voice. I swallow hard, then take out the red-stained knife from the pocket of my blue gingham dress and hold it up for everyone to see. People gasp. I watch the light bounce off the shiny plastic tip before throwing it on the table.

"I killed Harriet Conners because she knew the secret," I say as calmly as if I'm explaining that there's a slight chance of rain tomorrow. Then it hits me. My eyes widen, and I stare at the knife on the table like it's a cobra about to attack. I look at all the people around me and scream, "I killed Harriet Conners because she knew what happened. She knew what happened on the seesaw!"

I fall onto my knees. First I'm quietly weeping, then I am sobbing, and then I become fully hysterical and collapse flat on the floor. I can hear gasps of horror all around me now that everyone knows the truth. Tears pour out of my eyes, and my body writhes on the floor like a piece of bacon in a blazing hot frying pan. I pound my fists and kick my feet before coming back up to my knees and screaming at the top of my lungs, "I did it. I KILLED HARRIET CONNERS!"

For a few seconds there is complete silence. An undeniable tension saturates everyone and everything.

Then I hear a familiar creaking from above me. Without even looking up, I know the heavy red velvet curtain is beginning to fall. I don't stop crying until the gold fringe has hit the floor of the stage, and even then I give it one last good sob. As if on cue, I begin to hear the most beautiful sound in the world. Applause. The thick curtain muffles the thunder, but I can still tell the audience is going wild.

The lights flip from the warm, carefully constructed pools of illumination intended to highlight the drama onstage to the workday fluorescent lights that help the actors move around backstage. Intermission is only fifteen minutes long, and the entire set needs to change from classroom to courtroom.

I quickly get out of the way so the stage crew can get to work.

I wipe the stage tears from my eyes, and as soon as I do I notice real tears are at the ready just behind them. I can't believe this is my final performance.

I've been playing the role of Kimberly Ann Fortunato, the girl who lies, cheats, and schemes to cover up the murder of her best-friend-turned-middle-school-rival, Harriet Conners, in the off-Broadway production of *Seesaw for One* for the past three months. We were originally scheduled to run only for the month of July, but great reviews allowed us to extend our run through the end of August to Labor Day. My performance was often singled out. One theater critic wrote, "Isabel Marak Flores delivers a powerful and truthful performance that is *not* to be missed." I printed that review out and put it in my scrapbook. A review like that is something an actress dreams of.

Of course, the theater is a group effort. Everyone from the wardrobe mistress to the director has a part in creating the onstage magic, so no one artist can ever take credit for the success of a production. It's a team sport, and sometimes that's the part I like best—a whole group of artists pulling together to create something beautiful and meaningful for an audience. Still, it was wonderful to be noticed for my work. I was especially satisfied that the critic called my work "truthful." For an actor, that is the ultimate compliment. Acting isn't just pretending and playing dress-up. You must *be* the character. It takes discipline, dedication, and seriousness to do it well. My dream is to make it as a serious actress on Broadway one day, and each role brings me one step closer to that goal.

I only have a short amount of time between the curtain going down on act one and going up on act two, and I not only have to change, but I also have to do my vocal exercises and my meditation. While act one ends with my confession, act two is really where I put my dramatic skills to the test, so I need to be prepared.

"Isabel, that was amazing. Your best performance yet," Timothy Jackson says to me as I make my way backstage toward my dressing room, which is on the upstairs balcony. Mr. Jackson is the director, and he cast me in the role of Kimberly. He is the recipient of two Tony nominations and debuted his one-man show at Lincoln Center to standing ovations a few years ago. I respect him very much, and I'm grateful he believes in me.

"Thank you, Mr. Jackson," I tell him. "I've learned so much from you as a director."

"Well, I hope you'll continue to learn," he says.

"What do you mean?" I ask as we keep walking toward the upstairs dressing rooms.

Before he can answer, Hilda, the woman who coordinates the costumes, hair, and makeup, interrupts us. "Sorry, Mr. Jackson, I need to put her hair in a bun for the courtroom scene." There is not enough time during intermission to sit in a proper hair-and-makeup chair and be done up. Hilda grabs an actor where she can and does what she needs to do. Backstage is always chaos, but it is an organized chaos that I love.

"Oh, of course, go right ahead, Hilda," Mr. Jackson says. We both stop at the foot of the stairs that lead to the dressing rooms. "I probably shouldn't tell you anything until after tonight's performance anyway. Closing-night nerves, I guess."

Hilda steps behind me and starts brushing my hair, but I can't help wondering what Mr. Jackson means.

"Is everything okay?" I ask. "Did I do something wrong?"

"Oh heavens, no. Everything is fine. You haven't

done anything *wrong* at all. In fact, you've been doing everything right. Quite right indeed."

Hilda takes one last sweep with her brush, then twists my hair into one long piece and wraps it into a tight bun, which she fastens with a few bobby pins before lightly spraying the back of my head with some hair spray. Mr. Jackson quietly watches the transformation.

"You're all set, Isabel. Knock 'em dead." She pauses and adds, "Oh, wait. You already did that." She laughs at her own joke, then rushes off to get another actor ready for act two.

Mr. Jackson and I quickly climb the stairs to my dressing room. Once we are at the top, I look down at the stage and see that the army of a stage crew is in the middle of its orchestrated set change. A few men attach ropes to the walls of the classroom, and with a quick signal the walls suddenly float straight up past the balcony area where the dressing rooms are and into the theater's rafters. The walls of the courtroom pass the classroom walls like ships on a lake as they slowly descend from their perch above the stage. The crew hold their arms up for the arrival of the new scenery, prepared to safely secure it into place. Sometimes I think we should keep the curtain up during intermission so the audience could see how much work goes into the set change. In my opinion, it's as precise and challenging as everything else that happens onstage and, as my parents always remind me, "Where there is beauty, there is art."

"Isabel," Mr. Jackson says, "I wanted to tell you something rather important."

"Let me get the necklace for act two out of my dressing room," I say. My character chews the chain of her necklace while she's on trial. It's a little character quirk I developed after a few weeks of intense rehearsal.

I swing open the door to my dressing room, saying, "C'mon in Mr. Jack—" But as soon as I see what's inside, I freeze. How in the world did . . . ? I don't even finish my thought. I quickly pull the door shut, hoping Mr. Jackson didn't see what I just saw.

"Is everything all right?" he asks.

"Oh, fine," I say, quickly thinking of some excuse to keep him out of my dressing room. "I just remembered that old superstition. Never let your director in your dressing room on closing night. It's bad luck."

He tilts his head to the side and looks at me strangely for a second. "I thought I knew every theatrical superstition that exists, but I must admit, that's a new one."

I laugh nervously, hoping he won't ask to come in anyway.

"At any rate, I should let you prepare," Mr. Jackson says. "Normally I wouldn't distract you with this, but I want to make sure you have time afterward to meet someone very important. Do make sure you see me before you leave for the cast party. Won't you?"

Before I can ask who it is he wants me to meet, Sean, the stage manager, who I think was born with a walkie-talkie headset attached to his head, walks past us and without missing a step says, "We're at ten minutes until the opening of act two, Miss Isabel."

"Ten minutes, thank you," I say. It's protocol in the theater to acknowledge any time cue from the stage manager.

"I had better get back to my seat," Mr. Jackson says. "Break a leg. I know you'll be brilliant." He runs off down the stairs, and for a second I think about chasing after him to find out who this VIP is, but then I realize I have narrowly escaped exposing the secret in my dressing room. I have less than ten minutes to deal with the situation, do my meditation and vocal exercises, and get back onstage for the opening of act two.

CHAPTER 2

I open the door of my dressing room just wide enough so I can enter without anyone seeing what's inside, then shut the door tightly.

"Chernique!" I say, loud enough so she knows I'm alarmed but not so loud that anyone else backstage can hear. "What are you doing here?"

"Is that how you greet your best friend?"

"You know you're not supposed to be backstage."

"I've been backstage plenty of times. What's the big deal?" she says, waving her hand at me as she looks at herself in my makeup mirror. She's casually taking my lipstick out and testing it on the back of her hand.

"*After* the show, Chernique. After! I told you how Lorraine got in trouble for having her boyfriend backstage during intermission. What if one of the producers saw you? What if Mr. Jackson saw you?"

I'm not overreacting. *No one* is allowed back-stage during the performance. Sure, I've seen some of the adults break the rule, but when you're a kid working with adults, it means you have to follow the rules or else they treat you like a kid. I don't want to be treated like a kid, so I follow the rules. However, my best friend, Chernique, has never met a rule she didn't like to bend.

"How did you get past the stage door?" I ask. I'd never have the nerve to even try.

"Have you seen how adorable I am? Who is going to say no to an adorable little girl from Trinidad with chubby cheeks like these?" Chernique smiles in a way that perfectly shows off her pretty, round face. If I weren't so concerned about someone finding out she's in my dressing room, I'd laugh. "How could I stay in the audience when this could be one of the most important days of your entire life?"

"Don't be so dramatic," I say, grabbing the neck-lace out of the navy-blue velvet box I keep it in.

"Look, I know no one can play cool and calm better than you, but you *must* be freaking out. The letters were due out yesterday! I couldn't wait until after the show to find out what's going on. You've been dreaming about this since . . ." Chernique struggles to find the right word and then gives up. "Well, I don't know, but since we were six, this is the only thing you've really wanted."

She's right. I've wanted to be a student at the New York Academy of Dramatic Arts since the moment I learned it existed. The students at the academy take all the same classes regular students take, like algebra and English, but they also spend part of their day in classes dedicated to acting, movement, voice, and other theatrical subjects. Almost all the very best actors in the world started their careers there. Oscar winners, Tony winners, Seggerman winners—all attended the academy, and they all credit the rigorous training they received there as the foundation of their artistic success. Once I achieve my goal of making it on Broadway, I plan to become the youngest person ever to win all three prestigious awards, and the only way I can really hope to have any chance of doing that is to get into the academy. I prepared for weeks for my audition before finally having my parents record it and send it in. I've spent the summer waiting for the acceptance letter to arrive in the mail. The letters were supposed to arrive yesterday.

The only problem is, mine didn't.

"You know how slow the mail is in on the Lower East Side," I say.

"I think making you wait this long is cruel and unusual punishment." She takes the eyeliner I use onstage and puts some under her eyes, purposely smudging the line so her deep-brown eyes have a smoky look. "You are protected by the Constitution of the United States. I have half a mind to go up to where that fancy Mr. Tipton is sitting and tell him a thing or two."

As soon as I hear the name "Mr. Tipton," my eyes widen in shock.

"Back up. He's here? Mr. Tipton? The dean of the academy?" I ask. He's the man who single-handedly makes the decisions about who is accepted each year.

"Yeah. He's the guy on that TV show who asks actors all those weird questions like, 'If you were a breakfast food, what would you say to your glass of orange juice?'" Chernique deepens her voice and uses a stuffy accent for her imitation of Mr. Tipton.

"Yes. That's him."

"Well, he's sitting in the fifth row. You want me to accidentally hit him in the head with my program?"

"No," I say, and push Chernique out of my dressing room. "I want you to go back to your seat and be on your best behavior. I have to get ready." Even best behavior for Chernique is pretty wild. She sneaks out of my dressing room, and I take a seat in front of my mirror to put on my necklace.

Mr. Jackson said someone very important was here to see me after the show. Could he mean Mr. Tipton? Could he be giving me one last chance to get accepted to the academy? Is tonight's performance my last opportunity?

"We are at five until the opening of act two, Miss Isabel," Sean says as he raps his knuckles on my dressing room door.

"Five minutes, thank you," I say, loud enough so he can hear me on the other side of the door, and fasten the clasp of the necklace.

I shake the possibilities of who Mr. Jackson wants me to meet out of my head. I need to quickly change costumes and then do my meditation exercise and short vocal warm-up. If Mr. Tipton is in the audience, that means my performance has to be flawless. Until the final curtain falls, I'm not Isabel Marak Flores. I'm Kimberly Ann Fortunato, and I'm about to go on trial for murder.

CHAPTER 3

There are a few moments in act two when I look right at the audience as if they are the members of the jury. "It was an accident," I scream. "An accident." During that moment of hysteria onstage I *could* squint slightly to reduce the glare of the stage lights and sneak a direct glance at the audience to see if Mr. Tipton is in the fifth row. But I don't. Even if he is in the audience and I did see him, he would see me seeing him, and that wouldn't be good at all.

I maintain my focus until the final curtain falls. When it rises again for the curtain call and the houselights shine on the audience, I can't help but scan the people applauding to see if Mr. Tipton is there. Each member of the cast takes their bow, and as I am about to take mine, I see a thick gray beard out of the corner of my eye. I bend from my waist until my back is perpendicular to the floor, and on my way up I take a closer look at the fifth row and see that the gray beard is indeed attached to Mr. Tipton, who just happens to be applauding wildly. Behind him I see my parents and Chernique, who are also applauding wildly. Chernique has her fingers pressed between her teeth and is doing her trademark siren whistle to show her enthusiastic approval. Even though I often beg her not to do that because it draws so much attention, I secretly love it for the same reason.

After our curtain call, I want to join the other actors as they share teary good-byes and prom-ises to see one another again, but I'm too excited to find out who Mr. Jackson wants me to meet. Anyway, I'll see everyone at the cast party later. I walk directly to my dressing room and change from my costume to a simple pair of jeans and a black T-shirt. I take my hair out of the tight bun Hilda pinned up a short while ago and let my straight black hair fall around my shoulders. I look in the mirror and definitely like the sharp contrast between the dramatic makeup and my street clothes. The foundation makes my slightly olive complexion glow a bit, and the eyeliner makes me look a bit older and slightly more sophisticated, so

I decide to keep it on rather than scrub my face clean.

I walk out of my dressing room and down the stairs through the back of the theater toward the stage door. Before I can find Mr. Jackson, a plump middle-aged woman with curly auburn hair and gray roots, wearing a blue-and-white polka-dot dress, stops me very close to where Mr. Jackson stopped me during intermission.

"Hey, doll," she says. "You were sensational. Just sensational." Since she's backstage, I figure she must be related to one of the other cast members, but I don't remember seeing her before.

"Thank you," I say. I want to rush past her and find my family and Mr. Jackson, but it's rude to be so quick when someone is paying you a compliment.

"I'm Honey Arbuckle, and I'm sure you have a bunch of fans waiting for you out there, but if you ever need a job, give me a call." She thrusts her hand into a pocket of her dress and pulls out a business card, which she hands to me. It says HONEY'S KIDS in big block type, and underneath that, HONEY ARBUCKLE, OWNER.

Even though I have no intention of calling her,

I put the card in the front pocket of my jeans and thank her again. "Keep up the good work, doll," she shouts after me, and I wave good-bye to her.

There's a bunch of people waiting for friends and family members on the street outside the theater. I scan the crowd for Mr. Jackson, but my eyes only go a few feet, because he's standing with Mr. Tipton right next to my parents and Chernique.

I walk through the small crowd that has gathered to meet my family. My mom gives me a small bouquet of violets, my favorite flower in the world, and my dad hugs me and says, "You were fantastic, *mija*. I don't know how you do it. I cry at every performance."

"He does," my mom says. "But this time I came prepared." She holds up a small package of tissues. "You were just wonderful, *dragi*," she says. "You're so talented."

Mr. Jackson steps in and says, "Isabel, I hate to interrupt, but I would like you to meet James Tipton. He is the dean of—"

"The New York Academy for Dramatic Arts," I say, finishing Mr. Jackson's sentence.

Mr. Tipton laughs. "Well, then I guess we don't need a formal introduction. I was very much looking forward to meeting you tonight, but I'm afraid I've done something bad. Something very bad, and I hope you will forgive me."

Oh, no. Here it comes. I brace myself for the worst news possible but wonder why he would be so cruel as to tell me to my face that I'm not accepted. At least *not* knowing whether I got into the academy meant I could have hope, but actually knowing that I wasn't accepted has a sense of finality about it that I'm not sure I can handle. Still, the dean of the school has taken time to meet me backstage to personally tell me I was not accepted. It's very kind of him. I guess.

"As you know, the letters of acceptance were due to arrive yesterday, and I know for a fact that you did *not* receive one."

I look down at the ground. After crying onstage for two hours, you would think I wouldn't have any tears left in me, but my eyeballs feel like the Hoover Dam. "No, I didn't get one," I say.

Then he takes his arm, sweeps it across his chest, and digs his hand into his jacket. "You didn't receive one because I wanted to give it to you in person." He takes out a crisp white envelope with my name on it and hands it to me.

I carefully take the envelope from him. Once it is in my hands, I rip it open. I read the letter quickly, mumbling to myself as the words pass over my lips. "'Dear Miss Isabel Marak Flores. We are delighted to accept you as a student at the New York Academy of Dramatic Arts for the next academic quarter beginning in January. Please see the attached . . .'"

"I'm in!" I shout. I turn to my parents and Chernique. "I've been accepted. I got in!"

I can't believe it. I've finally been accepted after weeks of preparing for the audition, making sure each word of my monologue was perfect and that each movement of my body contributed to an understanding of the character. Then months of wondering and worrying if I made the right choices during the audition. Not to mention the years of dreaming about being a part of this prestigious school. I'm finally in. Starting in January, I will be a student at the academy, the New York Academy for Dramatic Arts.

I'm jumping up and down and don't even care that I look like a fool in front of someone as important as Mr. Tipton. I can't control my excitement. Chernique hugs me tightly, and my parents smile and congratulate me. My mom tells me how proud she is of me, and my dad nods his head in agreement, but when I look carefully at his face I can tell there is a hint of concern in it. My parents agreed to let me audition for the academy, even though the hefty price tag for the school was significantly out of reach for our family's finances. We decided we would figure out how to pay for tuition when and *if* I got in. Now that the *if* has disappeared and the *when* has turned to *now*, I can tell my dad is beginning to think about the cost of tuition.

"Yes, congratulations are in order," Mr. Tipton says. "Of course, I hope you don't mind that I wanted to see the look on your face when you received notice. But there is something else I must ask you, and I do hope you will agree."

I can't begin to imagine what in the world Mr. Tipton would want to ask me, so I just nod my head and listen.

"As the recipient of the Patricia Banner Scholarship for Artistic Integrity and Promise, I was hoping you would consider—"

Before Mr. Tipton can continue, my dad cuts him off. "Excuse me. Did you say scholarship? Did my daughter get a scholarship?"

Mr. Tipton looks flustered by the interruption. "Yes, yes. All the details are in the second letter I gave you," he says.

"Um, you only gave me the one letter," I say.

"I did?"

I hold up the single letter he gave me, and he looks at me as if to verify what I just said.

"So I did." He shakes his head slightly and looks around for a second, like he's almost not sure where he is. Then he pats his jacket pockets and says, "Oh, silly me. I forgot to give you this."

He hands me a second envelope and once again I rip open the seal, but before I can read the letter, Mr. Tipton explains, "The Patricia Banner Scholarship is awarded to the student who demonstrates the finest artistic integrity and achievement. Patricia is a personal friend of mine, and she reviews each student's portfolio herself before selecting a winner. It's only a partial scholarship, but it's quite a coveted award."

"You mean, Patricia Banner saw my audition video and reviewed my application portfolio?" Patricia Banner has been my idol since I was a little girl. She has won every major award that exists for the arts. She won her first Tony Award for her performance in *Cat on a Hot Tin Roof*, which Mr. Tipton directed and also won a Tony for. She has won two Oscars over the past decade, and last year she won her third Seggerman for her role in the political drama *I Will Not Stop*. The Banners have been part of the theater for generations. Patricia's great-grandfather, Louis Banner, was knighted by Queen Victoria for his contributions to the theater. They are the world's most respected theatrical family. It's in their blood.

"Yes, of course. Patricia was the one who suggested you play the part of Juliet."

Once again my parents, Chernique, and I look at each other in confusion. Mr. Tipton has a way of getting ahead of himself. I guess when you're an artistic genius, that sort of thing happens.

"In what show?" I ask, hoping he will explain further.

"In the benefit. That's what I came here to ask you. I'm directing a benefit to raise money for the Actor's Theater. This year we're doing a night of great scenes from the theater, and of course we can't omit the Bard now, can we? The closing scene will be from *Romeo and Juliet*, and we would like you to play Juliet. After all, the part was written for a girl about your age. It will be a light rehearsal schedule, and it's a good cause. What do you say, Miss Flores?"

Being directed by Mr. Tipton himself in the role of Juliet? I look at Chernique, who looks at me with her mouth open. Is there really anything to think about?

"Yes," I say, fighting the urge to jump up and down and kiss everyone within a fifty-foot radius. I didn't think anything could compare to the honor of being accepted to the academy, but this comes pretty close. I shake Mr. Tipton's hand and enthusiastically repeat, "Yes!"

CHAPTER 4

"*No,*" *my father says three whole days after I got* the best news of my entire life. "I'm so sorry. We both know how much you want this, but . . ." My father trails off, unable to finish his sentence. He turns on the faucet of the kitchen sink and lets the water run over his still wet paintbrushes. He has been in his studio all afternoon, supposedly working on a painting for his upcoming show at a gallery in Chelsea, but I know my mom was talking with him most of the time. They must have been discussing this school situation.

My mom gently puts her arm on my dad's shoulder, and she continues the talk. "We read the letter very carefully, and it's only a partial scholarship to cover the tuition for the nonacademic classes. We would still need to pay the other half of the tuition, and money is very tight right now. We don't want you to get your heart set on something that might not happen."

I sit at the counter next to the sink and watch the water turn a milky orange as it passes through the brush down the drain. I wonder if the water is taking all my hopes and dreams down the drain with it.

My heart is breaking twice over. First for me, because I won't be able to live my dream and attend the academy, but mostly for my parents, who feel so bad for not being able to send me. I don't want to cry in front of them and make them feel worse than they already do.

I move from the counter to the living room area and drop into the overstuffed armchair my mom reupholstered in recycled denim. I let the soft cotton fabric comfort me as I stare up at the unadorned steel beams on the ceiling of our Lower East Side loft. This building was once used to manufacture clothing before it was converted to low-cost apartments for artists and their families, so the high ceilings and frosted windows make it look more like a factory than an apartment. I look over at the horizontal row of windows on the south wall and notice a tiny crack in one of the square panes. I focus all my energy on that tiny crack to stop myself from crying.

My parents join me in the living room area and sit on the couch opposite me. "Please don't be upset, *mija*," my dad says. "We just want to be honest with you. But don't lose hope. There's still a chance I could sell a few of my paintings at the show in November."

"That's still months away," I say. With the list of credits I have on my résumé, you would think I might have earned enough money to pay for the academy on my own, but independent film and off-Broadway shows barely pay enough to cover the cost of cab fare to rehearsal.

I lean back in the chair and look across the room at one of my favorite paintings. My dad painted it a few years ago, when I was a little kid. It's almost four feet by four feet, and when I was little, I thought there was a whole happy world inside his painting. As I look at the warm tones that mix with bright, sunny strokes of color, I realize there are also tinges of grays and blacks in the painting, almost lurking beneath the surface. Today I can see the sadness in the painting.

My parents didn't have it easy growing up. My

dad grew up very poor in El Salvador at a time when violence was part of everyday life. The dream his parents had for him was that he would leave the country, so he could be someplace safe where he could focus on his painting. My mom grew up in Croatia and also experienced a lot of violence at a young age. She doesn't like to talk about the terrible things she saw during the war in her country, but she writes beautiful and passionate poetry about her happy memories from the country she was born in. Both of them have won grants and awards for their work, and I can't think of anything better than having two artists for parents.

However, having a painter and a poet as parents doesn't exactly make us rich in any monetary way. My mom teaches English at a local college, and my dad helps restore antiques at a shop downtown. That provides enough money for all the typical, normal things a kid could want or need. But luxuries like the latest video game console or cruises to tropical islands are not on the menu for our family. Usually it doesn't bother me one bit, as I have everything I need, if not always everything I want. Today, however, what I want is so much bigger and stronger than what I need.

"I've already called the department chair where I'm teaching this semester and asked her about some additional tutoring hours, but I'm not sure all these things combined will be enough," she says.

"We will try everything we can think of," my dad says. "We just wanted to be honest with you about everything."

"Thanks," I say quietly. "I understand." I'm disappointed, but I *do* understand.

Suddenly I hear my cell phone vibrating against the kitchen counter on the other side of the loft. I am thoroughly grateful for the interruption. "That's probably Chernique," I say. "I told her I'd meet up with her to go buy a new guitar string." I stand on top of the couch so I can see out the window to the street. I spot Chernique and wave to her. Since we don't have a buzzer, this is the system we've devised. I give my dad and mom a hug and a kiss and tell them not to worry about the academy. Of course, I'm still devastated, but I don't want them to feel bad, so I try to act as casual as possible. As I head down the huge freight elevator that opens into our living room, I do my best to leave my dark mood behind me, but it's harder than I thought.

I walk out of the building and cross the street to

meet Chernique. She is the most talented musician I have ever met. She sings, writes music *and* lyrics, and can play any instrument in the world, from the accordian to the xylophone. She once did a small concert in our loft where she played two instruments at once—the harmonica and the guitar. She is nothing short of amazing. She's also the most loyal friend a girl could want.

I have a great big smile plastered on my face, but before I even get to her side of the street, she says, "What's wrong?"

I drop my smile, and the sadness cascades over my face. "Oh, Chernique," I say, and without another word she gives me a hug. We walk down the street together, and I start to tell her about the conversation I had with my parents.

Chernique is not one to take no for an answer. She immediately starts coming up with ideas for me. "What about if you did more babysitting jobs? Hey, I could give you all the ones I have lined up for the fall. I have the Chengs twice a month and those brats who live on Thompson Street at least once a month. I could pass them both off to you."

I could never take Chernique's babysitting jobs away from her. Her family is just her and her mom.

They emigrated from Trinidad when Chernique was a baby. Her mom works at a hospital in the Bronx, and I know they struggle with money even more than we do. "Thanks, but I couldn't take your jobs away from you."

We walk down the block in silence, and as we're waiting for the light to change, Chernique screams, "I GOT IT!" More than a few people turn to look at her, but she has never had a self-conscious moment in her life. "Are those the same jeans you were wearing the other night? At the closing of *Seesaw*?"

I look down at my legs and realize that they are the same pair. "Yeah," I say.

"That's it! The answer might be right there in your pocket."

CHAPTER 5

I had told Chernique about my strange encounter with Honey Arbuckle during the cast party, but I had forgotten all about the strange offer of a job until Chernique reminded me about it right there on the corner of Stanton and Orchard Streets. If she hadn't, I probably would have washed those jeans with Honey's card in the pocket and forgotten about the whole thing entirely. When I'd asked one of the cast members if they knew Honey, I'd found out that she was actually a talent agent.

I'm already represented by one of the best theatrical agents in the world, Lenny Standard, at Artists International. Lenny started representing me after I booked my first major role in a small but important independent film called *Nora's Way*. I played Nora's self-destructive daughter, Nancy. I'd always wanted to act, but it wasn't until I booked this part that

I started taking it more seriously. Nancy in *Nora's Way* was my first really juicy role, and when Lenny saw the film, he called me into his office and offered to sign me there on the spot. That was at least five years ago, and since then he's been sending me out on auditions for everything from independent films to top-notch off-Broadway work like *Seesaw for One*.

"I don't need an agent," I told Chernique on the street corner. "I already have Lenny."

"But who knows? This lady said she had a job for you. She must know Lenny is your agent. It says so right in your bio in the program."

It's true. This woman must know that I already have representation, and there's no way an agent could even hope to steal a client from Artists International. It just wouldn't be possible. I assume Honey has me in mind for some other type of part-time work after school, like filing or something.

After school on Monday, I find a quiet corner of my bedroom, take out Honey's card, and call the number. I can't imagine what type of work she would want a kid like me to do for her, but if it pays well enough to help contribute to my tuition to the academy, I don't care.

Honey doesn't say much on the phone except that she's glad I called and that she'd be delighted to see me as soon as I can in her office. During our very brief conversation, I hear phones ringing and people talking very quickly and loudly in the background. It sounds like I've called the middle of Grand Central Station, so I can understand why she would need someone to help out in the office part-time after school. I take down her address and thank her for making the time to see me, since it's pretty obvious she's very busy.

The next day I take the bus uptown to her office, which is a few blocks from Madison Square Park in the Flatiron District. It's not an area I get to very often. Most rehearsals and auditions for the theater are in midtown, and that's also where my agent's office is located, so this is new territory for me. Honey's office is on the fifth floor of an office building off Broadway—the street, not the district. I take the elevator up and walk down a long hall to find a door with the words HONEY'S KIDS painted on it. Each letter is in bold black script but has been painted with golden yellow paint around it to make it look like it has been dipped in honey. It's pretty corny.

I knock on the door gently and wait. No response. I can hear people talking and phones ringing, so I knock again, only much louder. Still, no response. I knock again, and instead of using my knuckles I use my whole fist and pound so hard that I worry I might break the door. Surely someone hears me knocking. I wait a while longer. Still nothing. This place is in worse trouble than I thought. I decide to open the door and walk in.

When you walk into my agent Lenny's office, you're greeted by a pretty receptionist, who takes your coat and asks you if you would like still or sparkling water. There are modern black leather couches, which are designed to be looked at rather than sat on. The waiting area is quiet and dignified. The office I have just entered is more like a used car lot.

There is no waiting area, and no offices, for that matter. It's one big open room with desks and papers and headshots and folders piled everywhere. There are four desks scattered about the middle of the room and a person on the phone at each desk. Near the back corner of the room is one desk that is much larger than the others. Honey is sitting behind it on the phone. Her frizzy hair seems to go in every direction. The wall behind her is covered with headshots from top to bottom. There must be at least a hundred faces, from toddlers to teens, staring out at me. Honey laughs loudly and then jumps up from her desk and grabs one of the headshots, and I realize that each headshot is actually a stack of pictures, because once she pulls off the first one there's an identical one behind it. She makes some notes on her computer, hangs up the phone, and spots me standing near the door. She stands up, but instead of coming over to me, she just shouts very loudly, "Isabel! Isabel! Come on over!"

I feel more like a contestant on a game show than someone going on a job interview. I make my way through the office toward her desk.

"Kiddo. You were fabulous in *One for the Seesaw*. Just fabulous. I'm so glad you decided to come in today. So glad. It's great to see you again," she says, and thrusts her hand out for me to shake.

"That's very kind of you," I say, taking her hand. I don't tell her that the play was actually called *Seesaw for One*. She shakes my hand so hard I wonder if I'll need physical therapy. "Thank you very much, and thank you for seeing me today," I say as politely as possible.

"Are you kidding, kiddo? You are exactly what we need around—" Before she can finish her sentence, her phone rings. She doesn't answer it—instead she screams at the top of her lungs, "HEY, GARY! Can you pick up my line? It's Mel Bethany, and I DO NOT want to talk to her." A thin guy in his twenties in a plaid button-down shouts back, and Honey's phone stops ringing. "Anyway, as I was saying, you are exactly what we need around here."

"Well, I hope so," I say. "I'm not very good at typing, but I'm good at answering the phone and I can multitask, so filing and answering the phone at the same time is no problem."

"That's good to know, kiddo, but the only time I expect to see you in this office is when you're coming in to pick up a nice fat check or dropping off a muffin basket to thank us for making you so much money. And by the way—Gary is gluten free."

"I don't understand. How can I work as your receptionist and not come into the office?"

"Receptionist? Kiddo, I don't want to hire you as the receptionist. I want to be your agent. I want to represent you."

"I already have an agent," I remind her. "I'm represented by Artists International."

"I know, and that's very impressive. Lenny only represents the best of the best."

"You know Lenny?"

"In this town you can't spit without hitting an agent. Lenny and I go way back. Over the years I've represented a lot of his clients. If you sign with me, you'll still be signed with Lenny as well. He'll send you out on auditions for film, theater, and television. We call that the legit side of the business. I'll just send you out for commercials, print ads, and anything else you can book that can make a bucket of money. Artists International will be your legit agent, but commercially, you'll be one of Honey's Kids."

"Commercials?" I say out loud, but inside my head I'm thinking that I'm an artist, and the very idea of appearing on TV holding some juice box next to my face and smiling like a medicated chimpanzee makes me wince. Commercials are barely a step above those toddler beauty pageants. I guess it's all right for some people, but I see acting differently. Acting is about taking words on a page and portraying them in a truthful way that makes people feel something real. It's not about making someone *buy* something.

"Look, Isabel. You've got a great look that's really selling right now. Your dark hair is gorgeous, your caramel skin glows, and you have a smile that's warm and friendly. Not to mention the fact that you know how to memorize and say your lines. I think you could do very well. Very, very well."

She suddenly bangs her fist on the table.

"Oh, dang it all. I wish you were around two weeks ago. You would have been perfect for the Sweet Me spot."

"Sweet Me?" I ask.

"Yeah, it's some kind of new underarm deodorant for tween girls that smells like cupcakes or something."

The very idea of exposing my underarms on national TV makes me very uncomfortable, and the added idea that I would be spraying them to smell like carrot cake or something is even more disturbing.

"HONEY! IT'S MEL!" Gary screams from across the room. "She says she needs to talk to you NOW!"

Honey rolls her eyes. "I'd rather chew on a box

of staples than talk to this woman, but she casts more spots than anyone else in town. I've got to take this. You don't have to give me an answer now. I would love to work with you, so think about it and give me a call when you decide. K?"

I nod my head and get up to leave. Honey picks up the phone and immediately puts her hand over the receiver and says to me, "Boy, do I hate this woman." Then she moves her hand away and says into the phone, "Mel, my angel. How is my very favorite casting director in the entire world? Did you get the fruit basket I sent over?"

I let Honey finish her call and see myself out of the office. Honey gives me a small wave as I leave. I feel like I just left a backyard barbecue when I thought I was going to a fancy costume ball, or is it the other way around? I'm not sure.

CHAPTER 6

Even though attending the academy seems iffy at the moment, my parents said I could still be in the benefit, since raising money to help the Actor's Theater is a good cause and it doesn't really have anything to do with the academy, except for the fact that Mr. Tipton is directing. Our first rehearsal is tonight at eight fifteen.

At eight p.m. I ring the buzzer outside the stage door. The tiny speaker next to the door crackles, and a female voice with a thick Brooklyn accent says, "Actor's Theater. Can I help you?"

"I'm Isabel Marak Flores. I'm here for rehearsal." It feels good to be working on something again. It's only been a few weeks since *Seesaw for One* closed, but still I could feel my artistic spirit getting restless.

"Come in," the voice squeaks through the

speaker, and the door buzzes. I push it open and walk up a long flight of stairs to a small waiting room above the theater. Even though they are rarely painted green, the rooms where actors wait for rehearsal or to go onstage are always called greenrooms. I open the door to the greenroom, and a woman in overalls and a Yankees hat says, "Shh. Have a seat. I'll be right with you." She's sitting at a desk, watching a small TV. I sit down in one of the folding chairs in the waiting area. At first I think she is telling me to be quiet because someone is presenting their work onstage or in one of the rehearsal studios. Then I realize the TV she is watching is so loud that it can probably be heard in New Jersey, so I don't see how my whispered voice could disturb anything.

"And we'll find out the results after these messages," the handsome host of the TV reality show says through the tiny TV speaker. The woman turns to me and says, "Doncha just hate it when they do that?" She throws her hands up in the air. "Oh, geesh. I'm sorry for shushing you. I'm Gladys. I'm the back-of-house stage manager. I love this show, and I wanted to see who was getting voted off."

American Star has been on for a few seasons, and each year young people compete to see who will be the next big star. They sing and dance. They even do scenes from blockbuster movies, but you would barely call what they do "acting" in any artistic sense of the word. Still, Chernique and I have spent a few mindless nights tuning out and watching the teenagers compete. It's silly fun, so it seems a bit strange to have it on here at the Actor's Theater, where acting is taken so seriously. I bet Mr. Tipton would flip out if he knew.

The buzzer sounds, and Gladys responds and lets another person in. For a second I stare at the television with her, until I realize that she must have just opened the door for the other actor in the scene. That means the person I hear making their way up the stairwell is—I swallow hard before I even think it—my Romeo.

The heavy door from the stairwell to the greenroom opens.

"I'm Preston," he says as he enters the room.

Gladys introduces herself and then says, "You two are rehearsing on the main stage. Mr. Tipton will buzz me when he's ready for you."

"That's very kind of you," he says with a crisp

British accent, and sits down in the chair next to me. Gladys goes back to concentrating on *American Star*.

"Let's see," Preston says, turning to me. "The way it was explained to me, there are only two people in the scene, and since I know I'm playing Romeo, you must be . . ."

"Juliet," I say. "That's right. My name is Isabel. Nice to meet you." He extends his hand, and we shake casually.

I'm not the kind of girl to be boy crazy in any way. I'm too focused on acting and my career, but if I were the kind of girl who was boy crazy, Preston would be the exact type of boy I would be crazy for. He has this neatly combed dirty-blond hair that is perfectly parted on the side and gently falls over his tiny ears. I carefully glance over at him from my chair and can see that his eyes are greenish hazel and accented sharply by his thick eyebrows, which have a bit of an arch in the middle. His chin juts out from his face in a way that makes him look quite regal, and that British accent is dreamy.

I quickly remind myself that I am *not* boy crazy and that Preston is a fellow thespian and my scene partner.

"I do hope James isn't running late," Preston says, looking at his watch.

"James?" I ask.

"James Tipton, the director. He's an old family friend—known me since the day I was born."

"Oh," I say. "So you grew up here?"

"I grew up mostly in the UK, but I've had private tutors because Mother travels so much. But James insisted I attend the academy, since I'll be old enough next year."

"I've been accepted to the academy for next year too," I say. This is, of course, completely true. I have been accepted. I don't happen to mention that the small matter of paying for the academy is up in the air.

"What is WRONG with people? Honestly, what is WRONG?" Gladys shouts at the television.

"Is she all right?" Preston asks me, covering his mouth slightly so Gladys can't see, even though it would take a small explosive device to distract her from her show.

"I think so. She's very involved in her television program, *American Star.*"

As soon as I say the title, Preston makes a face like he swallowed a piece of laundry lint. "Ugh.

That show is vile. How in the world could anyone sit through an entire episode of that trash?"

"I'll tell you, that girl should not be voted out!" Again Gladys is talking directly at the television, as if she expects it to answer back. "Stacey Lyn has more talent in her little toe than the rest of the contestants have in their whole body."

Preston turns to me again and whispers, "That's the problem. It's all in her toe."

I giggle a little, but I'm careful not to laugh too much, since what he said was sort of mean and I don't want him to think I'm one of those girls who will laugh at anything a cute boy says. I try to change the subject from *American Star*. "What does your mother do that keeps her traveling so much?"

"She's an artist."

"That's so cool. My parents are both artists. My mom is a poet and my dad is a painter. What does your mom do?"

"She's an actress," he says.

At that moment Gladys's phone buzzes, and she looks down at the clipboard on her desk and says, "Isabel Marak Flores and Preston Banner the Third, right? Mr. Tipton is ready for you on the main stage now. You go through the hall to the stage staircase at the end."

Preston gets up, but I'm frozen in my chair. She called him Preston *Banner* the Third. This very cute boy is not just a cute boy, he's not just playing my Romeo, he's the son of the world-famous Patricia Banner. The woman who awarded my scholarship.

"Well, aren't you coming?" he asks cheerily. I get up slowly and follow him down the hall to the main stage.

It's always a thrill to walk onto a stage, even when the theater is empty and you're only there for rehearsal. For some people it's the lights, and for others it's the sound of the audience shuffling in. For me, it's the smell. There is a certain smell theaters have backstage—a combination of paint, hair spray, wood, and coffee that is magical. It makes me feel like anything can happen.

Mr. Tipton is at his director's table in the middle of the audience. The table is just a piece of wood from a former set that is set up over a few seats in the center of the audience. It has a small lamp and a laptop and is covered with books and papers. Mr. Tipton is known for doing a meticulous amount of research for his work. As soon as we enter the stage, he sees us, gets up from his desk, and starts walking down the aisle.

"I've been looking forward to this all day. My youngest performers doing the most challenging scene of the entire benefit. Welcome, welcome, Miss Isabel and Master Preston. Please join me downstage."

Despite being an older gentleman, Mr. Tipton is quick on his feet. He runs up the aisle and then jumps onto the stage and plops onto the floor and sits down in a shape that might be challenging for some yoga instructors. Preston and I sit down next to him.

"So, I want to tell you young actors an exciting idea I have. I am planning on doing this scene from *Romeo and Juliet* in the original verse, using an adaptation a friend of mine did."

"Well, that sounds wonderful," Preston says.

"Yes," I chime in. The truth is, this is going to be a very challenging scene and I'm a little nervous about everything. I've never performed Shakespeare before, and I hope I can do the work justice.

"Well then, let's get started," Mr. Tipton says. He leaps up from sitting and then stops suddenly. "Wait. Wait," he says as if his mind has changed channels. "I'm thinking of a color. Do either of you know what it is?"

I look at Preston and he looks at me. Mr. Tipton is known for his eccentric behavior, so I guess this is part of it.

"Yellow?" I guess, my voice quivering.

"Purple?" Preston says, his voice equally unsure.

"No. It was blue." Then he closes his eyes and shakes his head a bit and continues as if nothing strange ever happened. "Now as I was saying, we're going to be using a very rare and special adaptation of this scene from *Romeo and Juliet*. It is quite challenging.

"Now, you will both be required to do quite a bit of work on your own to achieve the type of artistic tone I'm looking for here. Are you both sure you're up for the challenge?"

"Absolutely," Preston says, and he looks at me like he might not mind working with me at all.

"Yes," I say, looking back at him.

"Then we have a lot of work to do. Let's get started by doing some breathing exercises and vocal warm-ups," Mr. Tipton says as he lifts his hands over his head and takes a deep breath.

CHAPTER 7

At the end of the rehearsal, Mr. Tipton goes over the schedule and reminds us about the important dates for the benefit, including the tech and dress rehearsals, which will happen on the day of the performance, the weekend before Thanksgiving. We are about finished when the doors at the back of the theater suddenly open.

"There are my two favorite boys and the brilliant young actress who is receiving my scholarship!" Even though it's a female voice, it is deep and booming. The sound echoes around the theater

Mr. Tipton and Preston smile and wave. My mouth drops open as the woman walks out of the darkness and into the light and I realize it's Patricia Banner. I had no idea she would be here, but of course I had no idea I would be in a scene with her son.

Mrs. Banner glides down the aisles of the empty theater as if it's a full house and every pair of eyes is on her. She looks exactly as she does in photographs. She has a long, narrow nose, and her dark-blond hair is pulled back tightly so her elastic face is the focus of her appearance. She is wearing what looks like a type of silk kimono that might also be a dress. A parade of brightly colored chiffon scarves float behind her like obedient and adoring fans. She climbs the stairs to the stage and air-kisses Mr. Tipton and her son before turning to me.

I open my mouth to introduce myself, and she holds up her perfectly manicured hand to stop me. "No. Don't speak. Don't introduce yourself. I know who you are. How could I not know who *you* are? You're Eileen, of course."

I don't know what to say. I'm not Eileen, but she's told me not to say anything, so I don't think I can correct her. Can I?

"You mean Isabel, dear," Mr. Tipton says gently, putting his hand on her arm.

"Of course, I do. I mean Isabel. It's such an honor to meet you." She curtsies and extends her hand to me. I'm not sure whether I'm supposed to kiss it or shake it. This is incredibly awkward. I touch her hand with mine in a weird type of hand-shake that very elegant hamsters might do.

"Thank you," I say. "And thank you so much for awarding me the scholarship. You have no idea what it means to me."

Mrs. Banner crosses the stage as if we are actually in the middle of a performance with an audience. "I know you will do us proud, dear. Unlike *some* scholarship recipients," she says, looking upward toward the sky like she's praying to some unseen deity. I look toward Mr. Tipton.

"Patricia simply means that we had a slight problem with another potential winner."

"Slight problem? It was a major embarrassment. She appeared on a reality television show, where she competed against other people by doing humiliating stunts like jumping into a hot tub of marshmallows and eating insects covered in dirt. I will not have the Banner name dragged through the mud—literally! That's why we're so happy to have an artist like you winning this award. Someone we know will maintain the artistic integrity of the Banner name. We can count on you, can't we?"

"Yes," I say. "Of course." My heart sinks into my stomach.

CHAPTER 8

"*Artistic integrity. You should have heard Patricia* Banner go on and on about the Banner name and how it was an honor to have this scholarship."

"Well, it is an honor," Chernique says, taking a spoonful of her yogurt parfait. I've insisted she meet me at our favorite diner, the Lafayette, so she could help me sort out my problem. We've been coming to this cozy diner since we were kids going with our parents after church. Now Chernique and I use it as a sort of hangout, since we started going to different middle schools last year when they rezoned our neighborhood. "I don't really see the problem," she says.

The fact that she doesn't see one doesn't help much. I swirl the ice around with the straw in my lemonade before responding.

"How can I go on commercial auditions as one

of Honey's Kids and maintain my artistic integrity? Honey said she would have sent me out last week on an audition for some cupcake-scented underarm spray for girls or something. Can you think of anything more disgusting?"

"Yes," Chernique says quickly. "Underarm-scented cupcakes."

"Thanks," I say sarcastically. "Now I'm stressed out and I want to throw up."

"I'm sorry," she says with a slight giggle, and then looks at me more seriously.

"If Patricia Banner even saw Honey's office, I think she might break down in tears or choke herself with one of her many flowing scarves."

"What's wrong with Honey's office?"

"Nothing is wrong with it. It's just that it's where dignity goes to die. Patricia Banner is very classy and high-end. She's like a diamond ring you would buy at Tiffany's. Honey is like the ring you dig out of the bottom of a box of Cracker Jack."

Chernique gives me her *look*. Her lips purse and her eyebrows sort of twist together and become one.

"What's wrong?" I ask.

"Just sounds like you're being a bit of a snob."

I hate the very thought of being considered a snob. "I'm not!" I protest. "It's just that they have certain expectations of me because of this scholarship, and I'm worried that if I sign with Honey they won't want me at the academy. I mean, what if I booked some embarrassing commercial for something personal like deodorant or something?"

"What's so embarrassing about deodorant? Please. It does a public service."

"But it goes under your arms and stuff." I wrinkle my nose and shake my head. "What would Preston say?"

"Okay. Hold it right there." She puts down her spoon and pushes the almost empty parfait glass away from her. "It has been less than twenty-four hours since you've been out of your first rehearsal, and you've mentioned this boy at least twenty-four times. That's a minimum of one per hour. I haven't said anything because you have a big decision to make, but what's the deal? Isabel, we tell each other everything. Remember?"

I've been holding back about Preston. When you have this incredibly cute boy playing Romeo opposite you in a scene, it's hard not to have a little bit of a crush on him. I've never really thought about "going out" with a boy before, but Preston Banner the Third could change all that.

"I am telling you everything. At least everything important. Preston seems like a very talented actor. I'm not surprised, since he *is* a Banner. They're one of the most important theatrical families in the world."

"Uh-huh," she says, knowing that I'm stalling.

"Okay, and . . . he's cute. He's *very* cute." Once I slip, I sort of fall down the mountain. "Oh my gosh, he has this perfectly groomed hair and this adorable accent." I gush a little bit. If you can't gush to your best friend, then who can you gush to?

"I knew it. You have a crush on him," she says.

"It's not like that *exactly*, but we'll be in rehearsal for the next few weeks, and he's been accepted to the academy for next year too."

"So if you were able to go to the academy, you'd be in the same class?" she asks.

"Yeah, I guess so," I say like I haven't already thought about that a hundred times.

"Well, then it sounds to me like you've already made your decision about calling Honey."

"What do you mean?"

"If you want to have any chance of going to

school with this Preston Banner the Third and attending the academy, I guess you had better book some commercials."

I put my lips on the straw of my lemonade and slurp up the last few drops before answering. "I guess I better make a phone call."

CHAPTER 9

"Honey's Kids. Please hold," a voice says quickly on the other end of the line. I'm not even able to get a syllable out before easy-listening music starts pouring through the receiver at an unreasonable volume. Three minutes pass, and finally a voice says, "Who are you holding for?"

"I'm Isabel Marak Flores. I'm holding for Honey," I say as politely as possible.

Then I hear the other person on the end of the phone scream, "Honey! Isabel. Line six."

There are a few clicks and then silence, and then I hear Honey's voice. "Hello, doll. I hope this call is going to be good news for both of us."

"I hope so. I'd like to start freelancing with you if you'd still like to work with me," I say.

"Absolutely. It's crazy here, but I got all your

contact information when you came in and I'll be in touch."

"Thanks. Thank you very much," I say, and hang up.

Well, that's that. I am officially one of Honey's Kids. It will probably be a few weeks before she calls me in again to see if I'm right for anything. I make a mental note to polish up my monologues this weekend in case Honey wants to hear them next week before sending me out. I could do a monologue from *Seesaw for One*, but maybe I should start working on something new. I wonder if I'll be ready to do something from Shakespeare by the time she calls. I know there aren't many commercials done in verse, but still, that would really impress her.

The very thought of Shakespeare reminds me that Mr. Tipton asked us to prepare a full character sketch for our rehearsal today. I look at the pile of textbooks on my desk and decide that I better start working on my homework now, and then I can work on my character sketch. I'll have plenty of time to work on a monologue for Honey this weekend. I take out my world history textbook, open up to the chapter on Mesopotamia, and start reading, but before I can even get through the first paragraph my phone rings.

The number looks familiar, but a name doesn't appear with it, so it must not be in my address book. Still, I'm sure I know the number, so I pick it up.

"Hello?" I say tentatively, not sure who will be on the other end.

"Hey, Isabel. It's Gary from Honey's office. I have an appointment for you. Do you have a piece of paper and a pencil?"

Since I'd just started doing my homework, I have both those items right next to me, so I say, "Yes," but I'm a little freaked out that I'm getting an appointment so soon. I'm not sure what my schedule will be next week. "I'm ready," I say, although that couldn't be further from the truth.

"This is at Mel Bethany Casting on Twenty-Second Street and Broadway. It's for Fruity Pops. The wardrobe is weekend casual. Your time is for three forty-five." I furiously write everything down and try to remember whether Fruity Pops are a cereal or a frozen dessert. I look over my scribbles and see that I didn't write down the day of the audition. I hope it's not too early in the week next week.

I'd like to have at least a few days to prepare.

"Have you got everything?" Gary asks.

"Yes," I say. "I only need to know what day the audition is."

"What do you mean?" Gary asks.

"I mean is it next Tuesday or Wednesday? I think Thursday would work best for me, but I don't want to be too much trouble. I could possibly do next Wednesday, depending on when I get the script."

"Isabel, doll," Gary says. I assume everyone in the agency follows Honey's lead and calls the clients "doll." "The audition is for today. Like in an hour and a half. The script will be at the sign-in. You can still make it, can't you?"

Today? In an hour and a half? Is he mad? How in the world do I have time to prepare?

"Should I pull you from the list?" he asks.

"No," I say. "I can make it. Thank you for the opportunity."

I hang up the phone and wonder out loud, "What in the world are Fruity Pops?"

CHAPTER 10

Gary said the wardrobe for the audition is "weekend casual," so I throw on what I wore on Saturday, since it was the weekend and it was casual. It's a blue denim skirt and a black, red, and white shirt with this repeating geometric pattern on it. There isn't much time to get to the audition, but still I stop in the Food Emporium grocery store near Union Square to find out what exactly Fruity Pops are. After a few minutes searching through the freezer section for some type of artificially flavored Popsicle, I finally ask a clerk, who points to me to the opposite end of the store. I'm relieved that Fruity Pops turn out to be a very respectable morning cereal. Although they are brightly colored pieces of puffed corn, they don't seem offensive enough to destroy the Banner name. With that small bit of knowledge, I head over to my audition.

I take the elevator up, and when the doors open, my mouth drops open as if in time with the elevator. I'm in shock. Usually when I attend an audition it's at a theater or a small rehearsal studio, and the director and casting director are sitting out in the audience in the dark. I rarely see any of the other girls auditioning. Maybe I see one or two, but they usually keep us pretty much spread apart. Here, I feel like I've landed on another planet.

There are girls everywhere.

All of them are about my age, and all of them are wearing about the same thing—a pair of simple light-colored pants and a solid pastel or muted primary-colored top. I look down at what I'm wearing. I must look totally out of place. My boldly colored top is the only print in the entire room. In addition to all the girls my age, there are women wearing khaki slacks, and all of them seem to be wearing some form of a sweater set in light blue, lavender, or mint green. It's like some type of uniform, and everyone is wearing it. *Everyone.*

"Do you need help?" a blond girl about my age in a teal-blue polo and khaki pants asks me. She's very pretty and looks very familiar. For a second I think I know her from somewhere.

"Hi," I say. "Do I know you?"

The girl smiles brightly, puts her hand on my shoulder, and says, "I get that a lot. I'm Brittany Rush."

"Isabel Flores," I say.

"You look new here," she says, eyeballing my outfit. "Is this your first audition?"

"Yes," I say, and then, "No. I mean yes and no, I guess . . . I mean yes." I've been on a ton of auditions for the theater, but this is the first time I've ever auditioned for a commercial, and so far the difference is pretty huge. "Does it show that much?"

Brittany scrunches her face and then leans in toward me and whispers, "In the future, I wouldn't wear such a bold print. It makes the camera buzz." She looks me up and down and says, "But you've got a great look. I'm sure you'll be fabulous. In fact, a few months ago I might even have locked you in a broom closet."

"Excuse me?" I ask. I hope she's kidding, but there's something in her eyes that makes me think she's only half kidding.

"Don't be scared," she says, laughing. "I'm just teasing, sort of. I used to be really, really competitive, but I've calmed down a lot since I've been back. I was in Hong Kong for a year, and my best friend Phoebe, well, she . . . anyway, it's a long story. Let me show you where you pick up the copy and where you sign in. It's all pretty simple. C'mon."

Brittany walks into the office through the large glass door. She shows me where the sign-in sheet is and then hands me a size card to fill out. It asks for my name, address, and every possible size you could imagine, from glove size to hat size. Brittany tells me to fill in the important ones and leave the others blank. We then walk down the hall, and I hand my size card to a woman who tells me to stand against the wall with my arms at my side. She takes a Polaroid of me that the camera spits out a second after the flash goes off. It has crisp white borders and a shiny, greenish-gray film over it. She waves the picture around a bit like she's trying to dry it, and slowly I see the solid color yield to an image of me standing against the wall. The woman staples it to my size card and hands it back to me.

Brittany asks to see the picture and scrutinizes it for a second, then hands it back to me. "It's fine for now, but in the future don't smile with your mouth closed. Ever. It makes casting directors think you have bad teeth," she says very matter-of-factly, and hands the card back to me. "And try to keep your eyes open."

I look down at the picture and realize that I'm in mid-blink. It looks like someone was shining a flashlight in my face. Not my most flattering shot.

We walk back over to the place where I signed in, and Brittany grabs some of the papers that are in a folder next to the sign-in sheet. "This is the copy," she says. "Sometimes they call them sides." I look at the pages and quickly realize that these are just other words for the script. "Relax and be yourself," she says. "They're going by call time, so it looks like you're going in next. My time is later, so I should be here when you get out."

"Thank you," I say. "This was really nice of you."

"No problem. I'm making up for some bad karma," she says, and gives me a little smirk. Somehow I think you don't have to go back that many lifetimes or even weeks to find the black mark in her past.

The door next to the sign-in area opens, and a guy in his twenties with a trim goatee and torn jeans pokes his head out. "I'll see Lisa Klein and

Isabel Marak Flores now, please." Brittany smiles and waves her hand, flicking her fingers in the direction of the door. My head is still spinning. A woman in one of the light-blue sweater sets gets up and walks into the studio. The guy with the clipboard looks around and then calls out, "Isabel Flores. Is Isabel here?"

"That's me," I say, and walk into the studio, not sure what to expect.

I follow the woman in the sweater into the room, but when I get inside I realize that calling it a room is a bit of an overstatement. It's really a large closet. There's barely enough space for a camera, a monitor, and someone to run the camera. Lisa and I stand against the wall opposite the camera.

"Hey, Lisa," the young man behind the camera says. "I saw your Pizza Fantastic spot the other day. It's hysterical. You and Phoebe are great."

Lisa smiles and says, "Thanks, Nick. They seem to be running them a lot. I keep telling my son that Pizza Fantastic is going to pay for his college education if they keep running wild spots like that."

My ears perk up when I hear this. That's exactly what I'm hoping I can do with Fruity Pops. I have no idea what wild spots are, but hopefully this is one of them.

"That's great. And hi, Isabel. I'm Nick," the guy behind the camera, whose face I can't see, says. Then Lisa and I introduce ourselves to each other quickly. In a theatrical audition you usually say your lines to a reader, someone who is behind a table, just reading the lines off the script to give you your cues. It feels sort of weird to be auditioning with another actor.

"Let's start with a clean slate, okay? Lisa, you first, then Isabel."

A clean slate? What in the world is a *clean slate*? We don't do clean slates in the theater, so I have no idea what he's talking about. I figure I'll watch Lisa and see what she does.

Nick points to Lisa, and the small light on the camera turns bright red. "Hi, I'm Lisa Klein, and my agency is Theory."

Then Nick points at me. I stare at the camera for a second before I say, "Hi, I'm Isabel Marak Flores, and my agency is Honey's Kids."

The light on the camera goes off and no one laughs or yells at me, so I guess I just did a "clean slate."

"So this is a real easy one, guys. They want it very fresh, very natural. Mom and daughter enjoying breakfast. Very simple. Did you get a chance to look at the copy?"

I suddenly realize that I didn't even look at it. I'm about to say no when Nick says, "Don't worry. There aren't many lines, and they're all on the boards." He points to a large piece of poster board that is clipped to a tripod right next to the camera. "Mom, you're in red. Daughter, you're in blue. Shall we go right to tape?"

Lisa shrugs, but I'm too busy reading the lines to give a response. I read through them quickly. I'm still not sure what they mean, but there isn't enough time to figure it out.

"Okay, here we go. Counting down in three . . . two . . ."

Lisa looks half at me and half at the camera and says, "And you know they're made with pure oats, so that means you're getting as much fiber as you would in a regular serving of bran-based cereal." She's so natural, so calm, and so normal that I don't even think the audition has started. I just think this very attractive woman is simply talking to me about her favorite cereal. It doesn't feel like she's acting in any way, but when I look over at the boards next to the camera I notice that everything she said is exactly on the poster board in red marker and it's now time for my line.

"But. It sure. Doesn't. Taste like . . ." I read right off the board, and then I realize Lisa talked right to me like she had known me since I was born. I'm reading the line like I'm giving a third-grade book report on the beaver. I clear my throat and start again. "But it sure doesn't taste like . . . Bran. Based. Cereal." I say each word as if it is its own sentence. It's hard to make something roll off your tongue when you've never heard the phrase used before. I can't imagine saying the phrase "bran-based cereal" to anyone, let alone my mother, at breakfast.

Lisa says her next line, and again it's effortless, and then the whole machine comes to a grinding halt as I try to read my line off the board and say it with some small level of emotion. I can feel Lisa and Nick get anxious each time it's my turn to speak. I start to feel like I'm terrible at this. It's nothing like acting. It's entirely different.

The whole thing lasts maybe five minutes, but it feels like five hours.

It's one thing to be humiliated. It's another to have your entire humiliation captured on video. Nick opens the studio door at the end of the audition, and I don't even say good-bye to him or Lisa. I dart out of the room, through the casting office, and down the hall, where I pray I will find a bathroom. Luckily, I do, and it's empty. I walk in, lock the door behind me, and cry.

I don't know what happened. I've performed in dozens of plays, I've been singled out for my performance in the *New York Times*, but four lines about stupid Fruity Pops make me look like I've never spoken in front of more than two people before. It was worse than that. I swear Nick thought I must have been an exchange student from another country, not even another country, another planet. Lisa said her lines perfectly, like she wrote them herself. I could barely read the words off the poster board, and when I could read them, I sounded like I was piecing them together phonetically.

On the second take Nick kept telling me to look into the camera as I said my lines, but that didn't make any sense to me, since I was supposed to be saying them to Lisa, who was playing my mother.

I guess it didn't matter that much anyway, because the lines were so strange I had to read them almost word for word off the cue card, so I wasn't looking at Lisa or at the camera. My face was buried in the cue cards. That can't be good.

That was truly one of the worst experiences of my life. I thought this would be so easy. I'd go on a few auditions, book some commercials, and be done with it. What does it mean that I can't even read a couple of lines off a cue card? Am I a terrible actress? It's just that this is so different from anything I've done before. I look at myself in the mirror and wipe the tears from my eyes. I examine my face carefully. My eyes are still red and a bit puffy, but at least they're no longer wet. I take a deep breath and walk out of the bath-room, ready to head out of the building. I turn the corner to go to the elevator, and I see the girl who tried to help me before the audition, Brittany.

"Hey, Isabel. How did it go?" I'm sure she can see that I've just been crying.

I don't say anything.

"Don't worry. First auditions can be really hard."

"Thanks for your help," I say. "Was your first audition a disaster?" I ask.

Brittany laughs and then stops herself. "I'm not exactly sure," she says.

"I don't understand," I tell her. "Did you block it out of your mind?"

"Well, it was for diapers, and I was about eighteen months old, so I don't remember any of the audition. But I did book the spot, so I guess it wasn't a total disaster."

As soon as she says the word "diapers," something clicks, and I suddenly realize where I must have seen her before. She's the baby on the Simply Dry Diapers logo. Of course, she's about ten years older now and, I'm assuming, no longer wearing diapers, but her eyes are still the same. Those are definitely the same eyes as the little baby who looks out from the box on the grocery store shelves.

"You're the Simply Dry Diapers baby."

"Guilty as charged," she says. "Look, I've been doing this forever, and I know it takes a while to get into the swing of things, but don't get upset." She looks down the hall to see if anyone is coming and then says in a whisper, "I have some great concealer in my purse. Let's go to the park, and I'll put some on your eyes. No one will ever know you've been crying."

"Thank you," I say, grateful that even if I didn't find a way to pay for the academy, maybe I've at least found a friend.

CHAPTER 11

Brittany and I walk over to Union Square Park together. It's only a few blocks, but she says at least half a dozen things that make me laugh out loud. She tells me that she has been in commercials since she was a baby, but she took last year off when her family lived in Hong Kong for a year.

"Coming back home was so hard," she says. "I mean, I was totally stressed out over the whole situation, but I learned not to take it all so seriously." Now she's really into drawing. "I carry a sketch pad with me everywhere," she says as we sit down on a bench. She opens her bag and holds out a rather large spiral-bound notebook with thick pages of unlined paper. "This is one of my favorites. The paper has this textured surface. Here, feel it." She opens up the book so I can feel the paper.

"Wow," I say. I didn't know that paper could feel so luxurious. "It's almost like fabric."

She flips through the sketchbook to show me some drawings, and they're good. Really good. I think about telling her that my father is a somewhat famous painter, but I don't want her to feel intimidated, so I just focus on her drawings.

"I love this one," I tell her, pausing at a drawing of a sunset over a lake. "You really are talented." She flips through a few more pages, and then I put my hand out to stop her.

"Who is *that*?" I ask as I point to a pencil drawing of an extremely cute boy with shaggy hair that sort of flops in front of his face and a smile that reveals he is not as innocent as he may look. Brittany blushes a bit and then looks down.

"That's Liam," she says coyly.

"I see. And who exactly is Liam?" I ask, knowing full well that she'll tell me he's more than a friend.

"He's a very special friend," she says.

"I thought so. How long have you two been together?"

She tells me that they had a rocky start but have

been together since the summer. "Is there a boy you like?" she asks.

I don't answer right away. I'm not usually the type of girl to open up right away to someone I've just met, but Brittany has been so nice to me that I can't help liking her. "Not exactly," I say. "But I did meet this boy recently and, well, I find him very interesting."

"Interesting? Hmm. Sounds like that could turn into something. If not, there are always a ton of boys at commercial auditions." I don't tell her that I'm really more focused on acting than I am on boys, but it's a shame I won't be seeing her at more auditions.

"Oh, I don't think I'm going to be going on any more auditions."

"Why not?"

"Are you kidding? I was a total disaster. I'm sure I'll never get called in for an audition again. I couldn't say my lines or look into the camera or away from the camera or wherever you're supposed to look. It was like someone sent a malfunctioning robot clone of me to the audition instead of a real live girl."

Brittany looks at me very closely. She's almost

like a computer trying to calculate the square root of pi or some other impossible number. She squints her eyes and then points at me.

"Move your bangs off your face and open your mouth like this," she says, opening her mouth like a lion showing off his teeth. I pause for second. I like Brittany and don't mind that she's a little bossy, but I feel strange doing this in the middle of Union Square Park. Still, I obey. I've always liked good direction.

"What's your background?" she asks.

"Well, I'm half Croatian and half Salvadoran."

She takes this information in and then tells me to stand up. She moves her fingers to indicate that I should do a full spin, then she motions for me to sit back down. After waiting a short while, she finally speaks. "Hmm," she says. "Listen, Isabel. I've been in this business forever, and I know what I'm talking about when I say this: You've got it."

"What?"

"It," she repeats. "That certain something that makes people want to book you. That quality that makes people linger on your face a second longer."

"I do?"

"You do. Unfortunately, you don't have any

idea what to do with it, but I think I can help you with that. I have a callback Thursday. Are you free in the late afternoon for a lesson?"

"Sure," I say. "You can come over to our apartment on the Lower East Side if you want."

"That's perfect. Here, put your address and number in here." She turns to a blank page in her sketchbook and hands it to me. "Do you have a full-length mirror?"

"Yes," I say as I start writing.

"Is it okay if I bring a friend?"

"Yeah, sure," I say.

"Let's see, it's almost five o'clock," she says, looking down at her watch. "How about this time on Thursday?"

"Sure," I say. "Five o'clock on . . . OH, NO!"

"What?"

"I'm late," I scream, and jump up from the bench. "It was great meeting you. I'll see you Thursday, but I have to go," I say. I wave good-bye to Brittany as I run with the speed of an Olympic sprinter.

CHAPTER 12

I run. I run like I'm being chased in a big-budget summer blockbuster action movie. I'm dodging tourists, leaping over puddles, and causing more than one yellow cab to honk their horn at me. I think a few cabdrivers might even have yelled unpleasant names at me, but I don't care. Isabel Marak Flores is never late for rehearsal. NEVER. I'm not about to let some silly commercial audition ruin my perfect record.

I arrive at the block the theater is on, and I'm sweating like an icy drink on a hot summer day. I'm so out of breath that I feel like my lungs might spontaneously leap out of my chest. I don't stop until my finger is on the buzzer to the backstage entrance.

"Hello?" I hear Gladys say. I can hear her TV playing in the background.

I try to catch my breath so I can form words and maybe eventually sentences. "It's . . ." I squeak out, but then have to close my mouth and breathe through my nose for a second. I look at my watch, and if I can just get in the door in the next forty-two seconds, my record will be intact. "It's . . ." I say again, but I can't seem to get my name out. I bend over and put my hands on my thighs to catch my breath.

"It's Preston and Isabel," a calm voice in a crisp British accent says from slightly above me.

The door buzzes. Preston opens it for me, and I walk through the door.

"Hello," he says. I walk up the steps more slowly than usual.

"Hi, Preston," I say.

"Are you all right?" he asks. "What happened to your . . . ah . . . everything?"

Blood and oxygen finally return to my major organs, and I suddenly realize how I must look. My hair is wet from sweat, I've been panting so my skin is red like a candy apple, and my shirt has come untucked from my skirt so I look like I got dressed in the dark. Not my prettiest moment.

"I was trying to get a workout in before

rehearsal," I tell him, and open the door at the top of the stairwell. "You know how important it is for an actor to stay in shape," I say as we reach the top of the stairs.

Gladys is in the greenroom at her desk. Her little TV is as loud as ever, only this time she's screaming at it. "What's wrong with ya? C'mon. C'mon." She seems to get more irate with each passing second.

"Are you all right, Gladys?" Preston asks.

"Oh, yeah. I'm fine. Do you guys watch *Make Me a Millionaire*?"

"I'm afraid I don't," Preston says, and I shake my head no.

"Well, this guy is about to lose all his money because he doesn't know who won the World Series in 2000. Can you believe that?" She goes back to staring at the television and talking to it.

"The World Series?" Preston whispers. "That's American baseball, right?"

"Yes," I say. "Have you ever been to a baseball game?"

"Never. I've been to quite a bit of football—or what you call soccer—but never baseball. Actually, I had my first American hot dog yesterday. From a guy with a cart in Central Park and everything."

"What did you think?"

"I think I won't be having another one of those. I'd rather eat at a real restaurant with a knife and fork." I love the hot dogs they sell from the carts in Central Park, especially with sauerkraut and mustard. It's one of my favorite meals. I guess it's just one of those quirky cultural differences. I'm sure there's a lot of food in London he loves that I would find disgusting.

"You were brilliant at the first rehearsal," Preston says. I love the way he uses the word "brilliant" like American kids use the word "great" or "awesome." He sounds like a member of the royal family, and then I remember he is—theatrical royalty.

"Thank you," I say.

"I can tell you really take acting seriously." He smiles at me as he pays me this compliment. It would be so wonderful to go out with a boy who understands how important acting is to me. I daydream about the possibility for a second.

"How long is yours?" he asks. I wonder if my daydreaming has caused me to miss part of what he said or if this is yet another British expression I don't understand.

"My what?"

He moves his backpack from his back to his lap and unzips it. He hunts around for a second before pulling out a few pages and showing them to me. The first page says, "Character Sketch."

"Oh, no," I say, looking down at the pages.

"Did I do it all wrong?" he asks. "Can you please help me before Mr. Tipton calls us in? Please."

"Preston, I'm sure what you have is fine," I say. I don't tell him that my stupid commercial audition made me forget all about doing my homework for rehearsal. Mr. Tipton made it clear that he wanted us to do a complete character sketch of our character before the next rehearsal . . . this rehearsal. He wanted us to write down everything about our character, from their favorite food to their favorite color. I had planned to do the assignment today before rehearsal, but after Gary called I completely forgot. This is so not like me.

"Mr. Tipton is ready for you now. He's in rehearsal studio C," Gladys says, and we walk down the hallway and into the studio.

"There you are," Mr. Tipton says as he shuffles some papers on his desk. He greets us with a huge smile, which mildly calms the panic that is sending butterflies crashing around my stomach. "I'm sorry for running a little late, but that is the prerogative of a director. A director can be late, but remember, an actor can *never* be late." My thoughts exactly.

Rehearsal studio C is like almost every other rehearsal studio I've ever been in. There is a smooth wooden floor and a wall covered in mirrors so the actors can see themselves while they're rehearsing or see other parts of the stage. Preston and I go to take our seats at the table in the center of the room, but before we can get there, Mr. Tipton says, "The first thing I want you to do is take out your character sketch. Take it out. Out. Out. Out. Right this second." He strokes his thick gray beard as he speaks.

Oh, no.

Preston already has his out, and Mr. Tipton takes it from him. I don't know what to do, so I open up my backpack and pretend to look through it to buy myself some time. The only thing that even remotely resembles a piece of paper is the stupid script from the Fruity Pops commercial. I take it out of my bag so I can throw it out immediately after rehearsal, but as I pull it out, Mr. Tipton comes over and grabs the script out of my hand, assuming it's my character sketch.

"Uh, Mr. Tipton," I begin, about to explain to him that the piece of paper he has in hand is in fact not my character sketch, but before I can, he has placed it behind Preston's.

"Today you'll learn my first rule of acting," he says, waving the papers around wildly in front of him. At first I thought it would look like I was lazy, but now I realize I'm actually going to be humiliated in front of both of them. "The first rule of acting," he says, then pauses and stares at each of us. He holds the papers up with both hands in front of his face and in one quick move rips them straight down the center.

"Break all the rules!"

He continues ripping the papers until they are in tiny little pieces. "I know I asked you to write up your character sketches for rehearsal today, but I only did that because I know you expected me to do that. Acting isn't about what you expect. It's about the unexpected." He then throws the pieces up in the air like confetti on New Year's Eve. They land all over the three of us. I look at Preston, and one piece of paper is even caught in the corner of his mouth.

"Now," Mr. Tipton says. "Take out your scripts, and let's really begin rehearsal."

I'm so relieved that my lack of preparation wasn't discovered that I can barely take in what Mr. Tipton has said. All I know is I won't be making any careless errors in the future.

CHAPTER 13

I've decided to turn my coaching session with Brittany into a small party. She's bringing her friend Phoebe, and I've convinced Chernique to come over as well. My mom is tutoring some kids after school and Dad is helping a friend set up his show at a gallery, so we'll have the whole place to ourselves. I convinced Chernique to help me make her mom's coconut puffs, since the first time you have someone over to your house you want to serve them more than microwave popcorn and jelly beans like some Charlie Brown Thanksgiving. The coconut puffs are a pretty simple recipe, since you start with premade pastry dough from the freezer, but the end result looks very complicated. The sweet, tropical flavor is perfect for an Indian Summer day in late September.

We take the last batch out of the oven after they

are browned to perfection and put them on the wire rack to cool.

"So are you having a rehearsal here?" Chernique asks.

"Not exactly," I tell her. "Brittany said she and her friend were going to give me some audition tips."

"But you've been on dozens of auditions. You've been on more auditions than anyone I know."

"The auditions I usually go on are totally different. I'm playing a role at those auditions. There's a character to study and understand. Like when I auditioned for Lily in *Tomorrow Never Comes*, I had read the entire script and I understood who Lily was before I even walked into the audition."

Chernique clutches her hand to her chest. "Oh, Isabel. You know how much I love that movie. We should watch it again, like, this weekend or something. Your final scene always makes me cry."

"Oh, you don't want to watch me in that. I was just a kid."

"You were so good in that film. Of course I'd love to see it again."

Brittany texts me that she has arrived and I head over to the window, where I see her and her friend, who is also blond and from a distance looks a lot like Brittany. I wave down to them and throw them the key to come up. I already texted Brittany instructions on how to use the key and the elevator.

The elevator doors open, and they both look around the space in awe. "Wow," Brittany says. "This place is really funky."

"Thanks," I say. Our apartment is definitely funky, and somehow I knew Brittany might like it. It's a large open loft space for the most part, and while it's home to me and my family, I don't think it's even close to being a traditional type of home.

"This is my friend Phoebe," Brittany says, and the blond girl standing next to her walks right over to me and hugs me, hard. Very hard.

Once she releases me from her grip, she looks me straight in the eye and says, "I'm a hugger." Her openness makes me like her immediately, and before I can even introduce Chernique, Phoebe has given her a hug as well. Chernique is a hugger too, so I know it's okay.

After the hug is over I say, "This is my best friend, Chernique, who is also a fabulous musician."

"What instrument do you play?" Phoebe asks.

"She plays all of them," I say.

"Oh, I do not. I mostly play the piano, drums, and guitar, but I also play the saxophone and started playing the clarinet a few months ago."

"That's impressive," Brittany says.

"I play a mean cowbell," Phoebe says. At first I think she's making a joke, but then I realize she's serious. It's actually pretty easy to imagine Phoebe rocking out on the cowbell.

"Let's head over to my room. We made some coconut puffs."

The four of us spend a few minutes devouring the snacks and talking about the latest celebrity breakup. I spend so much time with adults at rehearsals during shows that it's nice to hang out with girls my own age. Of course, I hang out with Chernique all the time, but this is different.

Brittany tells the story of how she and Phoebe were fierce rivals all summer and how they finally became friends after years of auditioning for the same parts.

"Anyway, let's turn on the TV and get started," Brittany says.

"Okay," I say, and grab the remote from the floor and immediately go to the channel guide.

"What do you guys want to watch?" I ask.

"Do you mind if I use the remote?" Brittany asks.

"Of course not," I say.

Brittany starts flipping channels and passes by program after program until she gets to a station that is on a commercial break. "Here!" she shouts, and walks up to stand next to the TV. Before she reaches the TV, however, I hear the very familiar Pizza Fantastic jingle, and then suddenly Phoebe's face appears on the screen. "Perfect," Brittany says, then points the remote at the TV and hits the pause button. Suddenly Phoebe's face freezes on the screen with her mouth half-open and twisted. "We will now have our first lesson."

CHAPTER 14

Brittany rewinds the DVR to the start of the Pizza Fantastic commercial. It's one I've seen before and have never quite understood. A family is in a rowboat, camping, and they somehow wind up ordering a pizza to their campsite.

"Let's look more closely at this commercial." Brittany looks around and spots an old Wiffle-ball bat leaning against the wall. She picks it up and says, "Do you mind?" I shake my head and she continues.

"First, let's notice what Phoebe is wearing."

Phoebe raises her hand, and Brittany calls on her. "It's a green T-shirt."

"Well done, Phoebe. So we have the first of some very important rules about commercial casting. Solids."

"Oh," I say, remembering the print that I wore

to my first audition. "So what I wore to the audition where I met you—"

Brittany doesn't let me finish my sentence. "Put it in your closet for school or going out on the weekends. You should never wear that to an audition again."

I look at Chernique, who shrugs and says, "Who knew?" I shrug also and write down the word *solids* in my notebook.

Brittany and Phoebe spend the next hour or so going over every detail of a commercial audition. I write down as much as I can in my notebook. I cringe when I hear some of their advice, because I know I did the exact opposite at my audition. Never look away from the camera. Never wear a dress unless the casting director specifically asks for you to wear one. Always wear to the callback what you wore to the audition.

"Now let's talk about your hair," Brittany says.

"My hair?" I ask.

"Well, it's absolutely gorgeous," Brittany says, and both Phoebe and Chernique nod. I've always been confident about my hair. Even though it's black like my dad's, it has some lighter highlights that I guess come from my mom's European side.

It's a little bit past my shoulders, and I usually wear it down and straight. I know Brittany is giving me a compliment, but somehow I feel there is a "but" coming.

"But," Brittany begins. There it is. "You *can't* wear it like that at an audition."

I quickly turn to look at myself in the mirror over my dresser. I've barely done anything to it today. It's just down and falling around my shoulders.

"At an audition the casting director wants to see your face and your eyes. Make sure you have your hair back when you go to an audition. Hair *is* important, but they want to cast your face, not your hair, unless it's for a shampoo or a conditioner. But even then, they still want to see your face, so make sure you have it pulled back or in a ponytail at the very least."

"But not in a French braid or a tight bun," Phoebe adds.

"Phoebe is right. Sometimes they'll ask you to put your hair down, and if it's up too tightly, you can't undo it quickly enough."

I'm getting a little confused. "Why do I wear my hair up if they're going to tell me to put it down?"

"Versatility. You have to be the 'you' they see you as, and you have to be able to show that very quickly."

That part's going to be hard.

"Oh," Phoebe says excitedly. "Don't forget to bring Vaseline to a callback."

"Vaseline?" I ask. "Do the studio lights make your lips get really chapped or something?"

Phoebe giggles. "No, silly. You put a thin layer on your teeth."

Chernique makes a face, and I do too. The idea of putting Vaseline in my mouth instead of on the outside of it is repulsive.

"I know it sounds disgusting, because it is," Brittany says. "But it can help. Callbacks can go on and on and on if they're matching up families or if the client and the director just don't know what they want. It can take forever, and the whole time you might be standing in front of the camera. And your mouth can get really dry. . . ."

"And what's the most important thing to do at an audition or callback?" Phoebe asks.

I want to say, "Look at the camera and wear a solid color," but I don't see how eating Vaseline can help with that, so I sort of have a blank look on my face.

Then Chernique, who has been paying close attention the whole time, says, "Smile!" Then she exposes her teeth in the biggest, goofiest grin she can conjure.

"Exactly," Brittany says. "The Vaseline can really help your mouth slide over your teeth, and it makes smiling easier. Believe me, you have no idea how many muscles it takes to smile until you've been smiling for, like, an hour without stopping. The Vaseline just makes it a little bit easier, and any advantage can be the one that helps you book the spot."

"Got it," I say, and write *Vaseline* in my notebook.

"But smiling is not actually the *most* important thing. Let's look at the Pizza Fantastic commercial again to see the *most* important thing to remember."

We've watched the commercial about six times already, but each time we watch it I learn something new. Phoebe is great, and the other people playing her family are equally as good. Sure, the entire premise of the commercial is totally inane, but for some reason I'm thinking about texting my mom and seeing if she can bring home a pizza for dinner tonight.

The commercial ends and Brittany says, "The

most important thing about auditioning for a commercial is that you need to be *you*."

This makes me very concerned.

"Phoebe books so many things because she's basically always herself. She doesn't try to be someone else. She just does herself doing whatever the audition calls for—from pretending to be fishing for pizza to shopping for a new computer."

Phoebe gets a little choked up hearing her friend talk about her this way. I like both of them, but they are pretty different. Brittany is direct and a little bossy. Phoebe is very sweet and a little unfocused. I guess a lot of friendships are based on opposites. Chernique is more free-spirited and spontaneous, while I'm more disciplined and a planner.

"The camera gets very close on you, and it can tell if anything is false. It has to be *you*."

Now I'm actually more concerned than I was before. At my disaster audition I was trying to figure out how to play the character of a daughter having breakfast with her mom. I never considered for a second the fact that I was playing some version of myself.

"But acting," I say softly, "is about taking on a role and becoming someone else. That's what I love about it so much. I love imagining what someone else's life is like from another time or another place. What did they wear? How did they talk? When you play a character onstage or in a movie, you can get totally lost in it. That's the challenge of acting. Where is the challenge in being yourself?"

Brittany and Phoebe look at each other. Brittany puts down the bat she has been using as a pointer and sits down next to me. "Trust me," she says, her tone a bit less demanding and authoritative. "Learning to be yourself is one of the hardest challenges you'll ever face." Something tells me that Brittany has learned this lesson the hard way.

"Oh, you know what spot I wish we could show her? Spa-la-la!" Phoebe says.

"The only way we'll be able to see that one is if we hop a plane to Hong Kong, and there's no way I am going back there," Brittany says.

I look at Chernique and she looks at me. We're both confused. "Did you have to shoot the commercial in Hong Kong?" Chernique asks.

Brittany explains that they shot the commercial in Queens, but reminds us that she lived in Hong Kong for a year and she missed New York every single second she was there.

"But you mean the commercial you shot here in the States only airs in Hong Kong?" I ask.

"Oh yeah," Phoebe says. "It happens all the time. They're for international brands that never appear in the US. I've done a bunch. The spa one was hard because I had to speak a few words of Chinese, and they didn't want to dub in someone else's voice later."

"But that almost never happens," Brittany adds. "Usually they use someone else's voice over yours or there aren't any lines."

"I did a chewing-gum spot that only airs in Brazil, and I don't even speak Spanish."

"They speak Portuguese in Brazil, Phoebe," Chernique says as kindly as possible.

"Well, there you go. I don't even know what they speak in Brazil, but my commercial airs round the clock, so it just goes to show you."

Then it suddenly hits me. "You mean, your gum commercial has never aired in this country?"

"Nope. I've never even seen it, but I know it gets a lot of play because my agent says the checks keep rolling in."

"So you get paid every time it airs in Brazil and you don't have to worry about it being seen by anyone you know?" I ask, unable to hide the excitement in my voice.

Brittany looks at me like I'm actually speaking Portuguese. "Personally, I try to avoid going out for the international brands. I mean, what's the point if no one is going to see you?"

That is *exactly* my point. If I could book a spot that airs in another country, I would never have to worry about Patricia Banner or anyone in the entire English-speaking world seeing it. It doesn't matter what the commercial is for. I decide right then and there that I'm going to have a quick chat with Honey about this as soon as possible.

CHAPTER 15

After school the next day, Honey calls my cell. Even though I'm anxious to speak to her, it takes me a few seconds to answer it, because I still have a rather painful memory of my last audition. I'm hoping she's not calling to tell me that this whole thing isn't going to work out. Now that Brittany and Phoebe have given me all these helpful pointers and I've learned that it's possible to book a commercial that doesn't even air in the United States, I'm pretty excited about finding a way to pay for school.

"Hello, doll," she says, her scratchy voice now more familiar to me.

"Hi, Honey," I say back as brightly as possible.

"I have an appointment for you Tuesday at three fifty p.m. at Betsy Barnes Casting. It's for . . ." Phew. At least she's not calling to let me go. I know I heard something about sending me on an audition.

However, the background noise on her end is very distracting. I can hear the other agents shouting on their phones and to each other.

"Did you say camping?" I ask. I didn't know they did commercials for leisure activities, but this world is so new to me.

"No! Hold on." I hear her covering the mouthpiece of the phone and yelling something to the staff that quiets the background noise. "Sorry, doll. It's like an insane asylum in here today. Not camping. It's for the CamPen. The pen that's also a camera."

"Oh," I say. That doesn't sound like anything too degrading.

"Don't worry about it. Half the auditions this month are for drugs that I have no idea what they do, let alone know how to pronounce them. They might as well be in a foreign language."

As soon as she says the phrase "foreign language" I think I have an opening. "Um, speaking of foreign languages—I was wondering if I could ask you a question."

"Sure, doll."

"Do you do a lot of spots for international brands? Because I was wondering: If any of those auditions came across your desk that you thought

I was right for, maybe you could send me out on them. I'd really like to try that."

"I do international stuff all the time, but to tell you the truth, those spots are pretty competitive, and I usually send out my more experienced girls." Dang. That means I'll have to humiliate myself in this country before I'm given the opportunity to do so in the international market. That really doesn't help my situation. "But," Honey continues, "you have so much theater experience that if one comes up that you're right for, I'll see what I can do."

"Oh, thank you, Honey!" I say, relieved. There's still hope for my plan! "I'll be at the CamPen audition on time, and I will do my very, very best. I promise."

"I know you will, doll," Honey says, and we both hang up.

CHAPTER 16

I want to at least get a callback for the CamPen spot so I can show Honey that I'm doing a good job. Then she might send me out on some international brands. As I walk across town to the casting office, I try to remember everything Brittany and Phoebe taught me.

When I'm about a block away from Betsy Barnes Casting, I stop in front of one of the chain drugstores and examine myself in the window's reflection. I look pretty decent for this audition, I think. Over my blue polo shirt, I'm wearing a pink-and-black-striped hoodie that I'll take off before I go into the audition. It's definitely too dramatic for a commercial audition, but I needed something to keep me warm on this chilly day. I take one last look at myself and realize my hair is totally wrong. I'm wearing it the way I usually do, down over my shoulders. Both Brittany and Phoebe told me to wear it off my face. I look at my watch and see that I have just enough time.

I run into the nearest drugstore and head directly to the health and beauty area, where I buy the cheapest barrettes I can find. When I get to Betsy Barnes Casting, I don't immediately sign in. I walk past the audition studios and down the hall to the secluded corner of the space where the bathroom is located. Luckily, it's empty, and I go directly in.

I'm in the smallest bathroom I've ever seen, and since I live in New York City, I see a lot of small bathrooms. But none of that matters as I take out the barrettes I just bought. I hardly ever wear barrettes, so it takes me longer than I thought it would to put them in so they don't make me look like I'm a puppet on *Sesame Street*. Finally I arrange them so my hair stays away from my face even if I shake my head a little.

By the time I'm done I realize I'm almost late for my appointment. I grab my bag, and with a rush of adrenaline, I push open the door, which swings out because the bathroom is so small. Then I hear someone yelp in pain.

"Argh!"

In front of me is a boy about my age, holding his head in his hands. I must have hit him when I opened the door, and considering the force I used, I must have hit him pretty hard.

"I'm so sorry," I say. "I'm really very sorry." He's still bent over, so I can't see his face. "Are you okay? Can I help you?"

"Yeah," he says. "Can you look around for one of my eyeballs? I think you might have knocked one out of my head."

I know he's only joking, but still I feel really bad. "Do you want me to get you some ice or something?"

The boy rubs his face hard and then straightens up and shakes his head like a dog coming out of a lake, trying to dry off. Once his face settles I realize he has an incredibly wide smile that sort of curves at the ends. He has short black hair and olive skin that is a bit darker than mine. The more I look at him, the more I realize he's definitely the type of boy a girl would call cute. In fact, I'd call him cute if I was that type of girl. Which I'm not. I don't think.

"My basketball coach always tells us to shake it off whenever somebody gets hurt during a practice, but I never actually tried it. Now I just feel dizzy. But don't worry. I'll be fine. Anyway, I already had my audition."

"Oh gosh, I should sign in. Look, I'm really sorry, but I better go," I say.

"Don't worry. If you're here for the CamPen spot, they're running behind. What's your name?" he asks.

"Isabel," I say.

"I'm Chuck," he says. "You must be kind of new. I don't think I've seen you at an audition before. I'd definitely remember you." The way he says it makes me a little nervous and a little excited. I don't think he means anything by it, and even though he is very cute, I think I already have a crush on Preston. And for a girl who has never had a crush on anyone, one at a time seems the way to go. Still there's something about him that is very, well, interesting.

"This is only my second commercial audition," I say. "I better go sign in. Sorry about your head and the door and, uh . . . you know, everything. See you around." I walk back toward where the studios are.

Once I'm a few feet down the hall, I think I

hear Chuck say, "I hope so," but I'm too far away from him to be sure.

I head toward the busy waiting area. Auditions for the theater are never this crowded. Usually my agent sends me on castings where they only see about half a dozen girls, and even then I've only been on a few auditions for plays where I've actually seen one of the other girls auditioning for the same part as me. Commercial auditions are more like what they refer to as "cattle calls."

I go to the sign-in sheet and see that Phoebe was here earlier, but I don't see Brittany's name on the list. I do, however, notice that Chuck's last name is Fulani and that he signed in about twenty minutes ago. I write my name down as clearly as possible, quickly fill out my size card, and go to the area in front of the studio where Polaroids are being taken.

This is another aspect of commercial auditions that is totally new to me. At a theatrical audition you submit a headshot and they know what you look like from that. At commercial auditions they take a new picture of you for each and every audition. At this casting office they print the picture they take right on your size card. There is a short line of girls and boys about my age. We shuffle along in line until it's our turn in front of the camera. Once in front of the camera, smile on. Flash. Smile off. Then we go to the printer, where we wait for our name to be called.

"Isabel Flores," announces an intern only a few years older than me. I raise my hand, and she gives me back my size card, which now has not only my measurements but also a freshly taken picture of my face.

"So you're Isabel," says a girl with chestnut-brown hair that has some wave to it. I wonder whether I know her from school or from somewhere else. She looks a little familiar, but at a commercial audition, everyone looks a little familiar.

"Do I know you?" I ask.

She shakes her head and smiles. "Geesh. I don't know what's wrong with me. Hi, I'm Cassie," she says. "I'm friends with Phoebe and Brittany. They told me that you might be here."

"Oh, right," I say. "They mentioned you." I look more closely at her and realize why she looks so familiar. "Are you on that Happy Family Cruises commercial?" I ask. I'm not sure whether it's cool to ask about these things at an audition, but I'm hoping the fact that I'm so new will mean I'm allowed to make a mistake or two.

"That's me," Cassie says.

"Wow! I love the dress you're wearing in that scene in the ship's ballroom. The one with the silver beads and sequins."

"I know," she says. "Isn't it great? I loved the way it sparkled in the light."

"That shoot must have been so much fun," I say. I expect Cassie to nod vigorously, but instead she sort of cocks her head to the side and bites her lip. Something makes me think it wasn't exactly the most fun she has ever had on set. I wonder if there's a story behind this but decide I should wait for her to tell me instead of asking.

"It was okay. Hey, did you get a chance to look at the storyboard?" she asks, quickly changing the subject. I tell her I haven't.

"Let's go grab a copy of the script," I say, and then quickly correct myself. "I mean the sides," I say, and remind myself that at a commercial audition the scripts are called "sides" or "copy." Why? I have no idea.

Since there are no lines to say in this commercial, there is simply a page that has a bunch of boxes on it that look like television screens. Each box has a drawing of what the creators imagine the commercial will look like. They have circled three of the boxes on the page for the part of Girl, so Cassie and I look at each one. In the first one a girl is in school studying and taking notes with an odd-looking pen. In the next box you see the girl using the pen to take pictures of a boy who is sitting on the other side of the classroom. In the third panel you see the girl sticking the odd pen into her laptop and downloading the pictures of the boy.

Cassie and I both finish and then look at each other. "Huh?" Cassie says. "Either I don't get it or this is really creepy. Is she stalking him?"

"I think so," I say, and we both laugh.

The door to the studio opens and a guy with a clipboard says, "I'll see Isabel Flores and Andy Simmons for CamPen right now in the studio."

"Neil's the casting assistant. He is *super* nice. You'll have no problem," Cassie says, and she squeezes my arm lightly for luck.

CHAPTER 17

I walk into the studio, followed by a boy about my age with curly strawberry-blond hair. Granted he's not as cute as Preston, or Chuck for that matter, but still very attractive.

"Let's get a slate first," the casting assistant says. I'm relieved that this time I know a little bit about what is going on. I stand on the line of masking tape on the floor and wait for Neil. First he points at Andy, who says his name and his agency and then turns to show his profile. "Hands!" Neil says loudly. This is a command I don't know, but I watch as Andy holds his hands up to the camera to show the front and back of them.

Next, Neil points to me, and I look directly into the camera and say, "Isabel Flores. Honey's Kids." I face the camera for a second and then turn and show one profile and then turn and show the other.

Neil says, "Hands," and without a second thought I simply raise my hands and show the front and back of them. I must have done it right, because Neil pauses the camera and comes out from behind it to explain the scene to us. "It's really simple. Isabel, you're sitting at that desk there, and Andy, you're at the other desk. Andy, you're just studying and oblivious."

Andy scrunches his nose and says, "What's oblivious?"

"Exactly," Neil says. "Just sit there. You'll be fine." Andy shrugs and slumps down in the chair. "Now Isabel, I need you to pretend to write with that." He points to a plastic fork sitting on the desk. I find it hard to believe that they couldn't find a pen to play the part of the pen, but I guess a fork is as good as anything else. Neil explains that I'm supposed to use the pen to take pictures of the boy without him knowing. He says, "It's like you know you shouldn't be doing it, but you're doing it anyway."

As soon as he says that, it all clicks for me. I think about the character I spent all summer playing. She murdered a girl on the playground. Now that is definitely something you're not supposed to do! I take a deep breath and prepare myself to become Kimberly once more, but before I can take a breath I remember that Brittany told me not to become someone else but to just be myself. Becoming Kimberly won't work, but how in the world do I just be myself, looking at a boy I shouldn't be looking at?

Then I remember the sort of exciting and guilty feeling I had when I ran into Chuck. It's easy to remember, so when Neil says, "Action," I think about my interaction with him and go through the motions of writing with the pen and pretending to take pictures on the sly. I wonder what it would be like if Chuck was the boy I was taking pictures of.

We run through the scene a few times, and each time I feel more comfortable being myself and not playing a character for a change. "Great," Neil says. "I think we got it. Thanks for coming in today."

Andy and I get up from our desks and walk out the door.

"How did it go?" Cassie asks as soon as I am out of the studio.

"Better than last time," I say. "I have to text Brittany and Phoebe. They really helped me."

"Those two are definitely the experts. If anyone knows how to book a part, it's them."

The door to the studio swings open, and Neil calls out, "Cassie Herold and James Polchin."

"It was great meeting you, Isabel. I'm sure I'll see you around," Cassie says before she goes into the studio.

I wave good-bye to her and make my way out of the crowded waiting area. Since I've been in the studio, the number of people waiting to go in seems to have tripled. All the boys are cute and athletic-looking, and all the girls are about my age and wearing solid colors with their hair pulled back. A few of them are with a parent or someone older, but most are on their own. I wonder which one of us will book the part. I wonder if it will be me.

Once I get outside I take a deep breath. The air has a chill in it, and I wish I had brought something warmer than my hoodie. I fold my arms across my chest and walk down the street, away from the studio. I thought this whole commercial thing was going to be a lot easier. I thought I would just hold up a juice box on camera, smile, and make a bucket of money. But it's not that simple. It's almost as hard as acting, which takes focus, concentration, technique, and, of course, talent.

I thought the hardest part was going to be keeping it from the Banners. But before I can even get to the end of the block, I realize maybe I spoke too soon.

CHAPTER 18

"*Isabel!*" *Preston says as he waves at me from down* the street. For a second I think about running in the other direction, but how would I explain that later? I keep walking toward him, praying he won't ask what I'm doing in a part of town that's so far from school, my house, and everything else in my life.

"What a wonderful surprise," he says. Preston looks so sharp in his gray wool cardigan over a collared white shirt with his usual crisp khaki pants.

"What are you doing here?" I ask. As soon as the words come out of my mouth, I realize that this is the wrong thing to say. Asking him what he's doing here will only prompt him to ask me the same question.

"Oh, I'm meeting my mum. She's getting a piece of jewelry that Sir Lawrence Olivier gave our family decades ago cleaned and polished at this little shop a few blocks away. What are you doing here?"

"What?" I ask as if I didn't hear him or some-thing.

"What are you doing here? You live on the other side of town, right?"

I try to change the subject by only answering the second question. "Right, it's not near here." I nod vigorously.

"So what are you doing over here?"

There is no getting around the question now, but I can't tell him I was at a commercial audi-tion. What would he think? And would he tell his mother? "Oh, I was just . . . um . . . I was . . ." You would think my acting skills would come in handy in a situation like this, but they don't. I flop around like a goldfish that has gotten out of its bowl. I decide I'd better tell at least some sort of truth.

"I came over here to buy these barrettes," I say, and point to the top of my head. Granted, these are the type of barrettes that you could buy at any drugstore anywhere in the world, but boys are typi-cally not aware of these things.

"Oh, I see," he says, cocking his head to the side and taking a closer look at my head. "Well, they look fetching. I had better run. Mother doesn't like to be kept waiting. I'll see you at rehearsal." He continues down the street. I stand still and watch him walk all the way down the block until he turns the corner and is gone.

"Phew!" I say out loud. That was a close one.

CHAPTER 19

Dinner on Friday nights at my house is always an event. My mom doesn't teach on Fridays. She stays home to work on her poetry, and my dad spends the morning painting. They take a break in the after-noon to prepare dinner together. My dad makes his trademark rice and beans, and my mom makes her Croatian goulash. You wouldn't think these two foods would go together, but they do, and the combination is absolutely delicious.

I help with dinner by setting the table and doing the dishes. I don't mind setting the table, but if I ever have any money left over once I pay for my tuition, I'm seriously investing in a dishwasher. Someone my age should not be walking around with dishpan hands. I grab the heavy pottery dishes out of the cabinet and place them on the table. The dishes were made by an artist my mom knows in Brooklyn.

They're made from clay she finds somewhere in a desert in Arizona, and she hand paints each one so no two are alike. Each one is a work of art, even though each one weighs about as much as a bag of bowling balls. I put the one with the lavender-and-white swirls on it at my seat, because it's my favorite.

My mom comes in and takes the lid off her goulash. The spicy-sweet smell wafts across the kitchen and over to the dining area. She dips a spoon in the simmering pot to taste it. She wrinkles her nose and says, "I think this needs a bit more paprika." Then she grabs a special jar near the stove that holds the sweet paprika she bought during her last trip home and sprinkles some into the pot. "That should do it." She puts the lid back on the pot and then comes over to the table.

"*Dragi*, your father told me you had an audition today after school? Was it for a new play?"

"Oh, no," I say. "Nothing like that at all. It was for one of those silly commercials. You could barely call it an audition. It's not like it was for anything important. It was for some dumb pen that's also a camera." I go into the kitchen to grab the silver-ware.

"But still, it was an audition. You got a chance

to practice your craft in front of people, and that's important."

"Well, sort of," I say. "It's sort of silly. That's all."

Then my dad comes out of his studio. "What's sort of silly, *mija*?" he asks as he goes over to the sink to wash the paint off his hands.

"Oh, I was telling Mom about my audition today and how it's sort of silly. I mean, it's just standing in front of a camera and saying or doing these things that must look ridiculous. It's not like painting a landscape or writing poetry or acting in a play. It's . . ." I trail off. I'm not exactly sure what it is, to tell the truth.

"What?" my mom asks gently, pushing me to think.

"Well, everyone is very nice at the auditions, and I told you about Brittany and Phoebe the other day. They're totally cool and everything, but I mean, they aren't artists." I feel satisfied with my answer. It's nothing against any of the girls I've met. "I mean, they go on auditions all the time. Brittany has probably been on more auditions than anyone in the entire world."

"Well, you think Chernique is an artist, right?" my mom asks.

"Of course," I say without hesitation. Chernique is one of the most talented and artistic people I know.

"What makes Chernique an artist in your eyes?" my dad asks as he takes the pot of rice and beans off the stove and brings it to the table.

"Well, she's creative. She's dedicated to her craft and always looking to improve herself," I say, and take my seat at the table.

My mom brings over her pot of goulash and says, "But the way you just described Brittany, it sounds like she is certainly dedicated to her craft if she has been on that many auditions."

"That's true," I say, and take a large spoonful on my mom's goulash.

"Sometimes being an artist isn't just painting, poetry, and performance. Art can take so many forms. You know who taught this recipe to me?"

I nod softly, because I know my mom misses her mother very much. "*Baka*," I say, which is Croatian for "grandmother."

"Exactly, and she was the most creative artist I ever met."

"Did she teach you to write poetry?" I ask. I don't remember any stories about her mother teaching her to craft words.

"No," my mom says, and laughs a little. "I don't think my mother ever wrote anything or painted anything in her entire life."

"Then how was she an artist?" I ask, taking some of my dad's rice and beans and putting them on the plate next to my serving of goulash.

"Cooking was her art," my mom says.

"Cooking?" I ask, not sure how cooking can be considered an art.

"My mother would cook the most creative dishes you could find anywhere in all of Yugoslavia. She mixed together ingredients that most people could never imagine. She was always trying out new recipes and making sure she was making the best possible food she could for her family. We were very poor, so she had to improvise, and her improvisations were on a scale with the great Miles Davis."

"I'll have to tell Chernique that." Miles Davis is her favorite jazz musician. She told me she gave a presentation on him in school last year.

"My mother taught me everything I know . . ."

"About cooking," I say, finishing her sentence and then taking a taste of the delicious goulash.

"No. She taught me everything I know about

being a poet. Yes, I apprenticed with great writers to learn about form and structure, but everything I know about being a true artist I learned from my mother."

My dad smiles at my mom and then at me and says, "You see, Isabel, being an artist isn't always just about what you put out in the world. It's about how you see the world."

I think very seriously about this for the rest of the meal, in between alternating forkfuls of goulash and rice and beans.

CHAPTER 20

After I finish the dishes, I meet Chernique in front of the old playground where our moms used to take us when we were kids. It's where we met. The city rebuilt it this summer, so all the swings and jungle gyms that we used to play on are gone. Even though the new equipment is very colorful and creatively designed, it still makes me sad when I realize that all the stuff we played on is sitting in a junkyard somewhere. I lean against the chain-link fence and watch the little kids running and chasing each other through the new tunnels and bridges.

I spot Chernique sitting on a bench and sneak up behind her. "Admit it. You miss the monkey bars."

"I'll admit I miss the monkey bars, if you admit you miss the seesaw," she says without turning around.

"Oh, the seesaw." I sigh wistfully, coming around the bench and sitting next to her.

"Yes, I'm sure you have many fond memories of your very first stage. You used to make me sit on the bottom so you could be at the top and act out any number of scenes. Don't you remember?"

"How could I forget? I did a rather brilliant Rapunzel at the age of five, if I do say so myself."

We both laugh. It seems like just a short while ago we were kids goofing around with stuff. I always liked to act, and Chernique was always singing a song or practicing some musical instrument. I look over at the spot where the row of seesaws used to be, and I think about how simple my life was as a kid. Everything seems so complex and overwhelming now.

"Should we walk to the East River? I bet some of the leaves on the trees over there have started to change colors. I have to be home early. You know how strict Trinidadian mothers are," Chernique says as we start walking down toward the river and away from the playground.

"Please. Like Croatian mothers are known for their lenient behavior. *Dragi*, make sure you are home on time," I say, imitating my mother's slight Croatian accent.

When we get to the park, we see that the large trees that line the river walk have begun to change from deep green to burnt butterscotch. The sun has begun to set, so it makes the water in the river look like it's covered in diamonds and sequins. For a few minutes we sit on a bench and stare out at the water and watch the gentle waves.

"I forgot to ask," Chernique says, breaking the silence. "How was your audition? Better than the first one, I hope."

"Much," I say, and explain how I ran into Cassie but didn't see Brittany or Phoebe, but that Phoebe had auditioned an hour or so before me. "Oh, except for the fact that I almost killed this very cute boy."

"You what?" Chernique asks, and knits her dark eyebrows together. I tell her all about Chuck and how I literally ran into him and how nice he was.

"He sounds cool," Chernique says.

"He is," I say, but even though I could go on talking about him, I think maybe I shouldn't, because Chernique already knows I sort of have a crush on Preston. Then I remember.

"So, who should be walking down Sixth Avenue after the audition, right down the block from the casting office, but Preston!"

"No! Was he auditioning too?" Chernique asks, knowing this can't possibly be the case.

"Please! You know Preston and his family would never EVER even think about being in a commercial. Not in a million years. He was on his way to meet his mom."

"Did you tell him about *your* commercial auditions?"

"Are you crazy?"

Chernique cocks her head to the side and gives me her patented *Are you crazy?* look. "Excuse me? You expect him to say . . ." Chernique clears her throat. "Pip. Pip. My dearie, is there any chance that you are disgracing my good family's name by going out on auditions for . . . oh heavens, I can't say it. *Commercials?*"

Chernique's upper-class British accent is so awful it makes me laugh. She sounds less like Mary Poppins and more like Mary J. Blige. "Don't laugh. I'm a musician. I'm not supposed to be good with accents." Then she laughs too, since we both know how ridiculous we must seem.

The laughter slowly fades and we sit staring at the water. It's only when my cell phone rings that the silent spell is broken.

"Oh no." Chernique checks her watch. "That can't be one of our parents. We aren't even close to being late."

"It's Honey," I say.

"Hello, doll," she says when I answer. "I knew you'd be a booker, and we are just getting warmed up."

"What do you mean?" I ask.

"I have a callback for you for CamPen."

CHAPTER 21

This time I remember my barrettes. I'm wearing the same simple outfit I wore at the original audition, and my hair is off my face. I thought about bringing some Vaseline to put on my teeth, but the thought of getting some of that disgusting goo on my tongue prevented me from doing it.

Phoebe and Brittany taught me that at a callback you don't need to sign in and get a photo taken again. Instead you go to the table in front of the studio and pick up the same card you filled out at the audition. I go over to the table and immediately see my picture on my size card, but before I grab it, I take a closer look at the other cards out on the table. I see Phoebe got a callback. That's great. But I don't see Cassie or Brittany in the pile. I hope that doesn't make either of them mad. I got the impression that Brittany is a girl who likes to win, but

Cassie struck me as a normal kid who just happens to go out on auditions.

I look at the other side of the table where the cards for the boys are laid out. I don't see a picture of the boy I auditioned with, but I do see a picture of Chuck Fulani. He looks as cute in the picture as he does in real life. I have this crazy feeling inside like I hope I get to see him at the callback, and I hope I don't, all at the same time.

Then someone puts their arms around me and starts squeezing. "Oh, I'm so proud of you I could burst!" Phoebe says. She wasn't lying when she said she's a hugger. Most people would consider this hug an attack, but one thing I've already learned about Phoebe is that she is serious about her hugs.

"Phoebe, I'm so glad you're here. Look," I say, and twirl around once. "No plaid, no dress, hair back, solid shirt."

"Wait, wait. Let me take a picture with my phone and send it to Brit. She's in class right now, but she'll want to see this." Phoebe looks through her purse for her phone.

"I hope she won't be too upset that she didn't get a callback," I say.

"Oh, she got a callback."

"But I didn't see her size card on the table," I say, confused.

"She got the callback, she just declined it. She started a class after school with my brother that she doesn't like to miss. Now hold up your size card and smile." I do as instructed, and Phoebe snaps a picture. "I'm gonna send this to her right now. She'll be so excited for you."

Neil, the casting assistant from the other day, walks by and says, "Hey. Taking pictures? That's my job. Now you wanna be in the commercials and do the castings. Phoebe, you'll be taking over soon."

"Hardly, Neil," Phoebe says, sort of blushing.

"If you're here for CamPen, we're about to get started, so make sure you have your size cards," Neil says to the group of kids in the waiting area, and then ducks into the studio across from where we had our initial audition.

"Brit has already texted me back. She says we should both break a leg."

"That's sweet," I say, and out of the corner of my eye I see Chuck walk in. I guess Phoebe sees him too, because she goes over and gives him one of her trademark hugs. They start talking, so I go to sit on the bench outside the studio. When they both come over to me, Phoebe introduces Chuck and me.

"We actually already know each other," Chuck says.

"You do?" Phoebe asks.

"Yeah, we sort of ran into each other at the first audition," Chuck says, and I'm a little grateful he didn't tell Phoebe about what a klutz I am. I'm also grateful that it looks like I didn't cause any permanent damage to him.

"Well," Phoebe says, "Chuck and I met this summer at a shoot for the Seven Sails amusement park. We had so much fun."

"Well, you did," Chuck says. "Phoebe was the lead. I was just one of the background kids on the rides. Turns out I like roller coasters a lot, but my stomach, not so much."

"Oh, right. I remember. We had to ride this roller coaster, like, fifty times before they got the shot," she tells me. "What was the name of that coaster?"

"The Screaming Demon," Chuck says. "It had three inverted loops and some serious gravity drops."

"Hey," Phoebe says. "We should all go out there

for Halloween. They keep the park open late, and it's all decorated with pumpkins and cobwebs. I bet I could get my parents to drive a bunch of us there some weekend."

"That would be awesome," Chuck says. Then he turns to me and says, "You aren't scared of roller coasters, I hope."

"Who? Me?" I ask. Honestly, I'm not sure whether Phoebe was including me in her plans, since maybe she was just talking about the kids who were in the commercial. But really, there is something about Chuck that makes me feel nervous inside.

Then Phoebe says, "Isabel, you have to come. It will be so much fun." Before I can say anything, Neil pops his head out of the studio and says, "Okay. We're set in here. I'll have my first two in now, and that will be . . ." He looks down at his clipboard. "Isabel Marak Flores and Chuck Fulani."

"Now?" I say. "Together?"

Neil looks at me with no idea why I'm asking these questions. He says, "Yes and yes."

"Here we go," Chuck says, and walks into the studio. I follow behind him.

CHAPTER 22

The studio is much bigger than the one we were in yesterday. About a dozen adults are in the area behind the camera, where there are a few tables and couches. Most are drinking coffee. There are two clear groups. One set of adults is all buttoned up, wearing dark suits and shiny leather shoes that look very uncomfortable. The other group is dressed much more casually in jeans, T-shirts, and funky sneakers in bright colors. It's easy to see that one group represents the business side of the commercial and the other group represents the creative side. A man in jeans and a baseball cap comes over to us.

"Hi, I'm Mike Michaels, and I'm gonna be directing this little spot. Here is what we have in mind." Mike explains the commercial in basically the same way Neil did the day before. I'm studying and taking pictures of a cute boy with my brand-new CamPen. The only difference is that the cute boy I'm taking pictures of this time is a cute boy I know, at least a little. Last time it was just a stranger. You would think the fact that it's actually Chuck I have to work with this time would make it easier, but it doesn't. It makes it harder.

We both say our names and our agencies to the camera. Chuck is represented by Theory, which is one of the most exclusive agencies in the city, according to Phoebe and Brittany. I go to sit at the desk to do my part, and Chuck goes to the other side of the room to be cute, which should really be no problem for him. The director yells, "Action," and we go through the scene. I try to do it exactly like I did at the original audition, but there's something about doing it in front of Chuck that makes me shyer and more reserved. The director yells, "Cut!" and walks over to talk to me privately.

"Isabel, sweetie. We loved what you did during the original audition. It was very clear from your facial expressions how you felt about this boy, but this time it seems a bit too subtle. Do you think you could brighten this a bit? Make it a bit bigger so it reads better for the camera?"

"Of course," I say. If there is one thing I can

do, it's take a note. I know how to use my acting skills to make a correction. Mike goes behind the camera and yells, "Action." This time as I go through the scene, instead of being nervous that it's actually Chuck I'm looking at, I remember that the CamPen is supposed to make me completely invisible. Chuck should think that I'm studying and taking notes with this oddly shaped pen, which at the moment is still a plastic fork. I use this to my advantage. I look at Chuck and go through the scene, but this time I pretend that he can't see me. Out of the corner of my eye I can see that both groups of adults are smiling and nodding, so I must be doing something right.

We do one more take, and then Neil says, "Thanks, I think they got everything they need." He opens the door, and Chuck and I walk out of the studio back to the waiting area.

"How did it go?" Phoebe asks.

"Isabel was great," Chuck says right away. I'm a little surprised by his comment, and my shyness creeps back a bit, because I know there is no CamPen creating an invisible wall.

"Thanks," I say. "He was also very good."

"All I had to do was stand there and look pretty,"

he says in a voice that shows he is clearly mocking himself. I like that even though he's cute—and he knows it—he isn't the type of guy to be cocky or stuck-up.

"Well, I'm sure you had no problem doing that," Phoebe says.

"He didn't," I say quickly and without thinking. As soon as I say it, Phoebe and Chuck both look at me like I said something a bit too revealing. Where is the CamPen to make me invisible when I need it?

Neil opens the studio door and yells out Phoebe's name and another name. "See you guys later," she says, and a boy who's not nearly as cute as Chuck follows her into the studio. This leaves me alone with Chuck again, which is something I like and don't like at the same time.

"So are you headed to the train?" he asks.

"No, I live on the Lower East Side. I'll walk home. Where do you live?" I ask.

"I live in the Bronx. I'm just gonna head over to the four train, so I can walk you to Union Square at least," he says, putting on his coat and backpack.

A walk to Union Square? That's at least five blocks, maybe six. Up until now we've had only the briefest of conversations. How am I going to think of something to say for five whole blocks? I smile, not letting on that I'm actually a bit terrified, and I put on my coat as we head out of the studio together.

Once we're out on the street, we walk side by side in silence for a few seconds, and then I ask, "So how do you really think it went for our callback?"

"Honestly? I thought you were great, but the truth is, you can never tell. I've had callbacks where I thought I knocked their socks off, and I didn't book. But sometimes I think I'm terrible and I book the spot. It's almost impossible to tell."

"Have you been in a lot of commercials?" I ask.

"A couple. Have you seen the one where the kids are playing basketball and they get tired and then the mom gives them each a glass of Brightday citrus juice?"

"Oh yeah," I say. "And then that little kid goes back outside and makes a basket from across the . . ." Before I can finish the sentence, I realize that the little kid is Chuck. "That's you!" I say.

"Yeah. It was a few years ago. That was my first commercial, and I totally booked it by accident."

"How did you book it by accident?" I ask. We stop walking at the same exact time as the light turns from yellow to red. Chuck turns to look at me, and the slight smile on his lips makes me turn and look away. I liked it better when we were walking side by side, since I could steal glances at him without him knowing. At least, I think he didn't know. The light changes back, and we join the other pedestrians and walk across the avenue.

Once we're on the other side, Chuck continues. "I was just playing ball with my buddies outside school, and this woman came up to me and gave me her card. She said she was casting a commercial and to have my mom call her. So my mom did. I booked the commercial, and I've been doing it after school and during the summer ever since."

"That's cool."

"It's fun sometimes, but sometimes it's not. The thing is, it helps my mom out a lot. My dad's out of the picture."

"I'm sorry," I say. Chernique's dad separated from her mom when Chernique was still a baby. She doesn't even remember him. I admire Chuck for being able to be honest with someone he barely knows about why he's doing commercials.

"It's all cool. I didn't really know him." Chuck looks down at the sidewalk and stops talking for a second. "What about you? Have you been in a lot of commercials?" he asks, changing the focus of our conversation.

"Oh, no. No, no, no. This is only my second audition."

"Really? You did a great job. I never would have guessed it."

"Thanks. I'm actually a real actor," I say. We are at a stoplight again, so Chuck turns to look at me, but this time I notice something in his expression like I've offended him a little.

"What do you mean, *real* actor?" he asks. The softness in his eyes that I glimpsed in my sideways glances is now gone. I suddenly realize how snotty I must sound. I don't mean to be.

"Oh, I didn't mean anything by that. It's just that I'm training to be a serious actor, and commercials are, well, you know, silly things to help make some money so I can attend the New York Academy for Dramatic Arts next year." I think back to the conversation I had with my parents during dinner the other night and wonder what they would say if they could hear me.

"I don't think they're silly," he says, and stiffly shoves his hands in his pockets.

Me and my big mouth. Why did I have to go and call commercials silly? We walk in silence for a few more seconds, and then we arrive at Union Square Park. "No," I say quickly, trying to repair the damage. "They're not silly. I didn't mean that. I mean . . ."

"I understand," he says, but I can't tell if he is blowing me off or if he really understands. "Well, I better hop on the train to get uptown. I'll see you later, Isabel."

"Yeah," I say. "Nice seeing you again." I try to sound as friendly as possible, even though I'm pretty sure he thinks I'm the most stuck-up kid in the world.

CHAPTER 23

By the end of the week, the first really cold day of October arrives, and the trees that line the street seem to have lost most of their leaves overnight. It's hard to believe that a few weeks ago everything was a vibrant green and the city was still muggy and hot. Now suddenly fall is here, and everything is different. I guess life is like that sometimes. Things seem like they will never change and then, "Boom!" in a split second everything is different.

When I get home, my dad is in the kitchen, washing out some of his paintbrushes in the sink. "*Hola, mija.* I can't believe the weekend is here. Your mom and I were thinking of making some popcorn with chili and lime and watching the Ken Burns documentary on jazz. Do you want to join us and see if Chernique can come? I know she'd like it if she hasn't seen it already."

"She has," I tell him. "She watched all twenty hours of it online. For a month last year she couldn't stop quoting it. But she has music rehearsal tonight, and I have to study."

"Pero es viernes!"

"I know it's Friday, but I have got to get these lines memorized by tomorrow or else," I tell him as I open the cupboard to get a snack. I try to think of what Juliet would eat for a snack, but I can't imagine organic gluten-free rice crackers would be on her menu. Still, they're the only viable option I see that offers even limited appeal, so I grab them.

"I see. Well, let me know if you want to me to run lines with you. I'll be in my studio cleaning up a few things."

"I will," I say, and head to my bedroom.

I put the rice crackers on my dresser and take out my script from my backpack. I have all my lines highlighted in yellow. This makes it easier to see which ones are mine. I spend about twenty minutes reading through the whole scene a few times. Since I'm alone, I read all the parts out loud to get a sense of the entire scene. Once I have that down, I go to my desk drawer to get an index card. When I'm memorizing a script on my own, without someone else to read the other parts, I use an index card to go down the page and cover up my lines until I have each one down perfectly. As I'm searching for an index card in my desk drawer, my cell phone rings.

I look at the number and see that it's Honey. I haven't even thought about the CamPen callback all day. I put it out of my mind, but now with Honey calling me it all races back to my head. What if I booked the spot? I can't believe it. Will this one spot be enough to pay for the academy? Then I think about how silly I had to act in the audition, staring at Chuck, and I cringe thinking about anyone actually seeing the commercial. Then I think, what if Chuck booked the spot too?

"Hello," I say into the phone.

"Hey, doll. It's Honey. I got the proverbial good news, bad news for ya."

"Oh, no," I say. "What's the bad news?" I figure let's just get that over with.

"Isabel, you didn't book the CamPen commercial. The casting director said it was really close and they absolutely loved you, but they decided they wanted someone with shorter hair."

"Oh," I say. I guess I'm disappointed, but part of

me is relieved also. "What's the good news?"

"I have an audition for you for a huge, and I mean HUGE, international spot that's scheduled to air in Japan and a few select Asian markets. It's for a new energy drink. At least, I think it's an energy drink. I'm not sure. It's for something called HappyWow. Ever heard of it?"

"Never."

"Well, everyone thinks it's going to be the next Pepsi or Red Bull or bottled water. This thing is racing ahead. I know it's a Saturday, but are you available tomorrow at one thirty at Double Doors Casting?"

I grab my calendar from my backpack and turn to the date. I have rehearsal in the morning, but after that I'm free. "I can make it."

"Great. Now they have some very specific requirements for hair and wardrobe. They want your hair pulled back in a ponytail for the audition."

"No problem," I say, writing down the instructions.

"And they want you dressed from head to toe in yellow."

"Yellow?" I ask.

"Yeah, that's what they said."

I think I have a yellow T-shirt somewhere, but yellow pants are going to be a challenge. I guess this means I'll be making a stop at the thrift store tonight. "No problem," I tell Honey. "I'll find something that will work, but why yellow?"

"HappyWow is an energy drink made from recycled banana or something. You are going in for the role of the lead banana."

"The lead banana?" I repeat. She must be kidding. I just spent the week with Mr. Tipton studying Shakespeare, for crying out loud. I am an actress. I'm a serious actress, not a . . . a . . . BANANA! Not to mention the fact that Patricia Banner would flip out if she saw me on TV playing a banana.

"And this will air in Japan?" I ask, just to make sure.

"Yeah, doll, they even flew everybody over from Japan for the auditions. Look, doll, the phones are ringing off the hook. Call me if something changes and you can't make it, but remember—this is huge. See ya, kiddo."

Honey hangs up, and I'm left staring at myself in the mirror. My mouth is hanging open. I can't believe I'm going on an audition to play the part of a banana. At least she did say this would only air in Japan, so even if by some long shot I book the banana part, no one will ever see it.

I open the door to my closet and stare at the jumble of clothes in front of me, hoping something yellow will pop out. Nothing does, so I close the doors and try to decide whether I should keep studying my script or head to the thrift store on Houston Street. The thrift store closes in about an hour, so if I head down to Rafi's Re-cycle-a-rama right now I can search through the five-dollar bins and be back with enough time to finish memorizing my script for tomorrow's rehearsal.

I grab my jacket from the coatrack and tell my dad where I'm headed. My life is a ridiculous combination of Shakespeare and bananas.

CHAPTER 24

Rafi's Re-cycle-a-rama is in a neighborhood between Soho and Chinatown that's only a fifteen-minute walk from our apartment. The store is known for the huge bins of used clothes that you can buy by the piece or even by the pound. When I was little, my parents would take me here and buy me a few pounds of clothes that I would use as "costumes" for the "plays" I would put on in our living room. I would develop a whole character around whatever piece of clothing I found. Once I found the top of a majorette's uniform, and I used it to play a talking spaceship that runs out of star juice before reaching its home planet. I'm sure the shows were dreadful, but my parents always encouraged me to play creatively and keep acting out stories, and that's how I decided I wanted to be an actress.

Rafi's used to be a supermarket in the seventies,

so the space is absolutely cavernous, and the owners have done very little to renovate it from its earlier function. There are still big signs on the walls that say things like PRODUCE and FRESH MEATS. The front of the store has all the high-end vintage like Pucci dresses and Dior suits, which cost almost as much now as they did when they appeared on the runway. I walk past the gorgeous couture and head toward the back of the store, where the cheaper clothes and the clothing they sell in bulk is located.

I spot the bins labeled FIVE-DOLLAR PANTS and head toward them. They are huge Dumpster-like objects that the store has painted in a variety of neon colors. I start with the one painted bright neon green and hope that something yellow will stand out quickly. I see a lot of pairs of old blue jeans and even a number of very interesting pants that must have been used in the military or something, since they have all these gold buttons and blue braid decorating them. My hand makes its way to the bottom of the bin without finding anything that will work, so I decide to head to the next bin, but I see some boy is already searching through it. He is bent over so I can't see his face, but he's looking very carefully, so it might be a while until I get a chance to do my search. Since he's being so careful, I tap him on the shoulder and say, "If you see anything bright yellow, let me know." Before he can turn around to see me I add, "It's for a costume." I don't want him to think some weirdo freak of fashion is harassing him for yellow pants.

The guy stops, pulls his head out of the bin, and stands up straight. It's Chuck. "You aren't about to play the role of a banana, are you?"

"Chuck!" I say with total surprise. "What are you doing here?"

"Well, HappyWow is not only made with bananas, it also uses limes. I'm looking for green pants." He rolls his eyes and shrugs.

I look at him, and it takes me only a second to remember how he made me feel the other day, because as soon as I look into his eyes I feel it again. Chuck has a certain something. There is no doubt that he is cute. His dark-brown eyes and his open smile are charms any girl would find compelling, but it's more than just his physical features. It's something else. He always seems to be having a good time, even when he's scavenging through a bin of old clothes, looking for a pair of lime-green pants. One look at his face and I can tell he has forgiven me for my last outburst about "acting," or at least he's forgotten it.

"Do you really see me as a lime?" he asks.

"Please, do you really see me as a banana?"

He squints his eyes and looks at me. "Turn around," he says, making a circle in the air with his finger. I bat my eyes and turn around like I'm in some sort of silly beauty pageant.

"Hmm," he says. "Well, I see you more as a pineapple or a stalk of fresh asparagus."

"Asparagus?" I say. At first I'm a little insulted. Who wants to be asparagus? But then I realize that both of the things he picked are actually quite visually interesting, so maybe he's even paying me a compliment.

"Oh, wait, come with me," he says, and quickly grabs my hand. He does it so fast there isn't really any time to think, so I follow him as he snakes his way past racks of old topcoats and stands of artfully arranged Easter bonnets.

"Where are we going?" I ask.

"Just wait," he says as we whip past a bin full of old varsity jackets to arrive in front of two mannequins, who look like they last saw a store window sometime in the fifties. He lets go of my hand, and at the moment all I can think is that we are no longer holding hands. Not that we were actually holding hands. We weren't. I mean we were, but we weren't. Actually, I don't know what I mean, and I'm not sure why he dragged me to the other side of the store.

"Look!" he says, pointing to the mannequins.

I examine them for a second. They are both dressed in vintage clothing from the seventies. One is wearing a tie-dyed rainbow top and pair of bell-bottom jeans. The other is wearing a lacy white top with daisies sewn all over it and . . .

"Yellow pants. You found them!"

"I knew I saw them somewhere, and here they are."

"Chuck, thank you. This has saved me so much time. I have so much to do tonight. You have no idea."

"Dang. You already have plans. I was hoping my reward would be going to a movie with me and some of my friends tonight."

I don't say anything. Movie. Chuck. His friends. I don't own the rule book on boy-girl dating, but if I did, I'm sure it would define this as an official "group date." At least I think it would. Why is it that I'm never sure of anything when I'm with boys?

"Sorry," I say, grateful for the fact that I don't have to explain my complicated situation with Preston. "But these pants are great." The size is right, and the price tag fits within my budget. "Even if they do look like they belong on a clown escaping from the Sunshine Circus," I say.

"They are pretty horrible, but they'll work for the audition."

"True. The only problem is, how are we going to get them off the mannequin?" I say.

"Well," Chuck says, "I can't do it. Can you see the headlines in tomorrow's paper? 'Young Boy from the Bronx Arrested for Mannequin Manhandling.'" He uses his hand to gesture with each word.

"We can't have that, now can we? I'll tell you what. You play lookout and make sure no one thinks we're doing anything weird, and I'll wrestle these pants off Matilda," I say.

"Who?"

"Matilda. Well, geesh. If I'm gonna take her pants off in the middle of the store, I had better know her name." Chuck laughs. "And grab me that," I say, pointing to a denim wraparound skirt that will be pretty easy to put on the mannequin quickly. Chuck hands it to me and then turns around to do the lookout. I quickly take off her pants and then even more quickly put the wrap skirt on her. "Thanks," I say. "All done."

"Don't mention it," Chuck says. "No, really. Don't mention it. I don't want people to know I go around disrespecting store mannequins."

"Technically, I was doing the disrespecting, but you were definitely an accomplice, so I'll keep it quiet. Hey, can I help you find your lime-green pants?"

"That's okay. I got some time to kill before I have to head over to the movie, and I know you've got plans so . . ."

"No way. You found me the world's most hideous yellow pants. The least I can do is return the favor. How do you think you might look in bright-green paisley?"

"Like I escaped from a commune in California."

"Great. So we'll both look like we escaped from something. Let's head back to the bins."

I start walking over to the bins, and Chuck follows me. I know I should go home and study my lines, but for just this once I can choose fun over work.

CHAPTER 25

By the time rehearsal arrives on Saturday morning, I have all my lines completely memorized. Of course, after running into Chuck it was difficult to really concentrate, but I did my best for as long as I could. Then I got up extra early to make sure I knew every line.

I ran through them with my dad during breakfast. "*Mija*," he says, "I don't know how you memorize all these words and in English. Ay! I would never be able to do it. *Nunca*, I tell you."

"But Dad, English is your second language. It's my first."

My mom, who has been listening to us rehearse the lines, says, "I'm impressed too, *dragi*. Your English is wonderful."

"Mom, you only say that because English is your *fourth* language," I remind her. Besides speaking the language of her homeland, Croatian, my mom also speaks French and Spanish. In fact, she met my dad when they both enrolled in an English class at the Lower East Side artists' collective.

"Well, still you work very hard, and we are both very proud of you."

"Thanks," I say, "but I better get going. I don't want to be late for rehearsal." I grab my backpack from the couch and unzip it quickly to make sure I have everything. My script, bottle of water, and usual supplies like pencils, lip balm, and chewing gum are right next to my neatly folded yellow T-shirt and bright yellow pants. Mr. Tipton always ends rehearsal on time, so I should have no problem changing before my audition. The last thing I want to do is meet Preston looking like I'm an Easter egg.

I kiss both my parents good-bye, and my dad says, "Wait. Take a banana with you in case you get hungry." He grabs a particularly bright one from the bunch in the basket on the counter. I don't have the heart to tell him that the last thing I want to eat today is a banana, so I just take it from him, thank him, and put it in the side pocket of my bag.

• • •

For the first time since we've started working on this scene for the benefit, rehearsal goes smoothly. I don't feel unprepared or lost. Granted, the entire rehearsal is about blocking, and that just means the actor is told where she moves to when she says each line. The important thing to do during a blocking rehearsal is have a pencil and write down everything the director says. At the end of the rehearsal Mr. Tipton tells us both that we did a good job, and I feel a huge amount of pressure evaporate as Preston and I leave the rehearsal studio and head toward the greenroom to exit.

"Well, that wasn't as grueling as usual," Preston says as we reach the stairs.

"No, but blocking is always easier than anything else."

"True." Preston puts his script in his bag and then turns to me. "There is something I wanted to ask you." He clears his throat and moves his hand over his hair to smooth it down even more. "My mother is planning a little get-together to watch the broadcast of the Seggerman Awards. They're airing on some cable channel here, so she thought it would be fun to throw a party, since she can't attend in person this year."

"The Seggerman Awards?" I say in disbelief.

His mother won her first Seggerman five years ago for her role in *Staunch Women*. It was an R-rated film, so my parents didn't let me see it, but I read every review I could find and studied every photograph that exists. According to the reviews, *Staunch Women* was a tour-de-force performance by Patricia Banner, who displayed every emotion from birth to death on the screen. When she was nominated, she was the hands-down favorite to win and of course, she won. The Seggermans are the single most respected award in the film community. It's much more distinguished than winning an Oscar and more like the Cannes Film Festival. It would be absolutely thrilling to watch the Seggerman Awards in the company of such an esteemed actor as Mrs. Banner. Not to mention her adorable son.

"Well, do you think you might be able to join us for the broadcast?"

"Yes. I would love to."

"Well then, it's a date," he says, and right before he opens the door to the greenroom, he kisses me on the cheek. It's just a little peck, and it happens to land much closer to my ear than my cheek, but still it's the first minute in my life that involves both mouth-to-face contact and the word "date."

I don't move.

I need to process what all this means. But before I can even wrap my mind around everything, Preston walks on and passes through the green-room as he heads down the stairs. "I had better run off. I'm meeting Mother for brunch."

Once I hear the door slam, I'm dropped back into reality. I'll think about all this later. At the moment I've got to transform from upstanding thespian to energetic banana. I grab my bag and head into the bathroom. Luckily, on Saturdays Gladys is off, and a college intern who is too busy on her laptop to really notice anything is stationed in the green-room. In the bathroom, I quickly change out of my supercute magenta-and-pink-striped sleeveless top, which falls just over my hips and is perfect for the often saunalike conditions of the rehearsal studio, into my bright-yellow ensemble. I look ridiculous, but if a four-dollar pair of pants that look like they fell off the sun is what it takes to book an international commercial that will bring in the bucks, so be it. I was smart enough to bring a jacket to cover up most of the outfit, but when I look at myself in the mirror, my dark-purple hoodie covers up the T-shirt, but my bright yellow legs stick out even more now. I look like I jumped off the game board for Candy Land. Luckily, the audition is not that far away. I head out of the bathroom and through the greenroom to the stairs. I open the door to the stairs and make it halfway down when I hear the outside door buzz and then open.

"Oh, Isabel, you're still here. I forgot my—oh, dear! What happened to your legs?"

I freeze. My body is in suspended animation. Preston just saw me a few minutes ago wearing a simple pair of dark-blue jeans with my striped top, and now I look like Big Bird in a hoodie. How am I going to explain this?

"Oh, hello again," I say, as if my legs look perfectly normal.

"Did you change your . . ." Preston begins, but before he can say anything, I jump in.

"Oh, these. Well, these are my other pants. I had to change into them because you know, I'm . . . uh . . . volunteering today at that soup kitchen for the homeless on the Bowery."

"And you can't wear normal clothes there?" he asks, and it's a perfectly fine question. I unfortunately do not have an answer for it.

"Oh, you can, of course," I say very slowly, so I

can think of an answer. "It's just that the homeless have such a hard time of it, and I like to wear something that will brighten their day," I say as quickly as possible. It's like the words are a runaway train spilling out of my mouth. Preston just looks at me.

"That's very cool," he says, and it makes me think he has bought my ridiculous story.

I make my way past him. I get myself safely on the other side of the door and peek my head back in so the offending pants can't be seen and say, "Nice seeing you today. Call me later. Bye." I pull my head out into the cold autumn air and slam the door behind me.

I have no idea what Preston must think. Even if he didn't buy my story about brightening the lives of the homeless, at least it's better than letting him know I am auditioning for the part of a banana.

CHAPTER 26

The elevator door opens at Double Doors Casting, and it looks like a life-size box of Skittles has exploded. There are dozens and dozens of kids my age, each one dressed in a distinct color of the rainbow. I assume each color represents a different fruit in the recipe for the HappyWow energy drink. The atmosphere is much more circus than serious audition, but that doesn't surprise me. I take off my hoodie, revealing my bright-yellow head-to-toe wardrobe, but instead of sticking out, I actually fit in. A girl dressed in bright red jeans and a bright-red sweatshirt walks past me. "Excuse me," I say, and tap her on the shoulder. "Do you know where we're supposed to sign in?"

She looks me up and down and then says, "Either you're here for the banana role or you're a bumblebee missing her stripes." She's dressed as ridiculously as I am, so I think she is definitely in on the joke.

"I'm a banana," I say. "Nice to meet you . . ."

"That sounds like the beginning of a knock-knock joke," she says.

I'm not sure whether she's a cherry or a strawberry, but before I can answer, she says, "Cherry," then sighs. "All the girls who are a little rounder, like me, are here for Cherry." She is an adorable girl with an ample figure and bright-orange hair that she has tamed into two pigtails. "All you beautiful tall girls are here for bananas. I'm sure you'll meet some nice lime and have beautiful smoothies together while I'll be stuck with some grape."

Just then a chubby boy with glasses, dressed head to toe in purple, comes up to her and says, "Hey, Donna. I didn't know you would be here." He looks at her like he thinks he's a real player, but you can tell pretty quickly he isn't.

Donna rolls her eyes and says, "I told you at the Open Office shoot that you're not allowed to speak to me unless you're reading from a script. Now exit." She points her whole arm in a direction away from the elevators, and the poor boy doesn't say a word. He smiles glumly and walks away.

"Don't worry," she says to me. "That's just Howie." Then she looks from side to side and down the hall to see if anybody is listening. "Isn't he adorable?" she asks.

"Sure," I say, confused. "But you—I mean—"

"Oh, I know, but sometimes with boys you just have to do that." She shrugs and then points in the opposite direction from where she sent poor Howie. "Over there is where all the bananas are going. I better head back."

"Thanks, Donna," I say. "Oh, and by the way, I'm Isabel."

"See you around, Isabel," she says.

I walk down the hall, and as I turn the corner I suddenly see an army of girls my age dressed in every shade of yellow you can imagine, from daffodil to goldenrod. Some girls are even wearing yellow hats, and when I look down, I see that two or three of them are actually wearing yellow shoes. Where they found yellow shoes, I have no idea. At the other commercial auditions I've been to, there have been a lot of girls, but nothing compares to the size of this crowd. There must be at least three dozen girls trying to sign in and prepare for the audition. I take a deep breath and prepare myself for what I'm sure will be a grueling, if not completely bizarre, experience.

I slowly make my way through the crowd of yellow clones and find the sign-in table. Before I can ask if I should sign in before filling out my size card, the woman behind the table gets up from the chair she was sitting in. She places the chair to the side of her and stands up on it. She cups her hands to her mouth in a makeshift megaphone and yells, "Girls. Please fill out a size card and then return it to me to get your number. Do not, I repeat, DO NOT go in without getting your number. They will not see you today without a number. They will call you in groups of eight and by your number. Make sure you have a number."

Great. How do I get a number? I thought by my third audition I would understand most of what's going on, but this number thing is new. I look around at the other girls and realize that most of them have a piece of notebook paper with a number on it taped to their yellow shirts. It looks like the type of number a runner wears in a marathon, and I assume that this is the number the woman who is standing on the chair is so concerned about.

I wait for her to get down from her chair and

take her seat back at the table. When she is seated, I sign in and ask for a size card. Before she hands it to me, she says, "Make sure you get a number before you go in."

"Yeah, I understand," I say. I wonder if I should use something stronger than tape to attach the number to my shirt, since they're clearly so important.

I fill out my size card and find the guy who is snapping Polaroids for the audition. It's like a scene from a horror movie. A guy with a short ponytail that has almost completely come undone is surrounded by a swarm of yellow girls who each want their photo taken so they can get their number and audition. There is no official line. Each girl waves her size card at him, and the frazzled guy takes her picture, hoping to calm the frantic demand. I stand off to the side, hoping things will quiet down, but after a few minutes I realize they won't, so I push my size card in his face, hoping he will choose it and take my picture. Eventually he does, and I show my gratitude by mouthing, "Thank you" and smiling as kindly as I can. I think he understands, but it's impossible to tell because the swarm doesn't let up.

I take my photo and size card and go back to the table where the woman is handing out numbers. She checks off my name and hands me a long piece of tape and uses a thick black Sharpie to write the number 217 on a piece of paper, which she then hands to me. "Two hundred seventeen?" I say with a bit of shock. "Do you mean you've had over two hundred girls audition for this part?"

"No, no, no," the woman says, and I feel a bit more relieved. I know this is a big spot, but there is no way I could compete with over two hundred girls. The odds would not be in my favor. Then the woman continues, "We've had over two hundred girls just this morning. We already had five hundred girls yesterday. Now take your number and move out of the way." I do as I'm told but watch as the girl behind me gets the number 218 written on a piece of paper.

I can't believe they will see almost a *thousand* girls for this commercial. I guess I basically have no chance of booking it. I feel like a domino at one of those record-setting events, waiting to topple over and join the thousands of other already fallen dominoes. For a second I consider throwing my number in the trash and going home. But I can't.

This is the spot that could help pay my tuition, and even though it involves one of the most humiliating scenarios I've ever heard of, the fact that it will only be seen in Japan makes me feel a little better about the whole thing.

The door to the studio opens, and a short woman with a clipboard yells, "I need bananas 210 to 217 in here now. If you do not have a number, you will not be seen."

They are not kidding around with these numbers. Since they're ready for me to go in, I follow the other seven bananas into the room and hope that it will be over quickly.

CHAPTER 27

"Bananas! Bananas!" the woman with the clipboard shouts while clapping her hands. The other seven girls look toward her and obediently give her their full attention. I stare at the other girls, shocked that they don't find the fact that this woman is calling us bananas very odd. If it weren't for the fact that there's already a camera in the middle of the room, directly pointed at the group, I would think I was on a hidden camera show.

"Bananas, this is Hiro Fukishima. He is the director of this commercial *and* the creator of the HappyWow energy drink." A tall man with long black hair that almost touches the tops of his shoulders bows and smiles at us. I assume he's Japanese. "This is his interpreter, Miko." A woman with an extremely short haircut, who seems to come up to just above the director's belly button, bows quickly. The other bananas applaud, and once again one banana stands alone. He makes an energy drink. Big deal. It's not like he invented the lightbulb or a cure for some painful disease. Still, it's only polite to join the others in applauding, so I do.

Mr. Fukishima bows and then starts yelling in Japanese. Now, I am not familiar with Japanese at all. I've been to a few sushi restaurants, where I believe I've heard it spoken, and maybe it's one of those languages that is just very loud, but still, even if it is, Mr. Fukishima is *yelling* by any standard. Miko says, "Mr. Fukishima says you are all happy bananas. You are happy, happy bananas."

Well, I'll admit one thing: This whole experience is bananas. Where's a rim shot when I need one?

Mr. Fukishima screams a bit more, and then the interpreter says, "You are very happy to be part of the drink HappyWow. It is a very good drink, a very proud drink."

Proud? That must have lost something in translation. Pride is not exactly what I feel at this moment, and how in the world is liquid proud?

More screaming from Mr. Fukishima, and then

from the interpreter, "Wait for the music and then dance. Happy bananas dance."

All the other girls are looking at Miko and Mr. Fukishima very intensely, like this is a completely normal day. Like they spend most afternoons dressed like a sun-bleached traffic cone while someone screams at them in another language. Sure, this happens all the time.

Mr. Fukishima points to a young Japanese boy with green-and-purple hair that sticks up like he tried to electrocute himself and failed. The boy hits a button, and then "music," for lack of a better word, comes blasting out of a pair of small but powerful speakers next to him. It must be the HappyWow jingle, but it sounds like something they would play to torture people.

The lyrics go something like this: *"Tang. Tang. Happy. Clang. Clang. Wow. Tang. Clang. Happy wow. Happy wow. HappyWOW! Tang. Taaaang."*

The other girls seem to think this is a normal jingle, because no one follows through on my first instinct, which is to run out of the room screaming. The woman with the clipboard fiddles with the camera and says, "Make sure your number is facing the camera. I need to see your number." They are really obsessed with these numbers. I pat my chest to make sure mine has not accidentally fallen off.

All the other girls start jumping up and down, laughing and dancing. For the first five seconds I don't move. I can't. I mean, it's one thing to be dressed like a banana. It's another thing to be a dancing banana. I have to draw the line somewhere. But then I look at these girls just dancing with their little banana feet like the floor is on fire, and it starts.

Oh, no. This can't be happening, but it is.

I'm getting the giggles. I can feel it. I can feel it start pulsing through my veins, and then it makes its way almost instantly to my brain, and I can't stop the waterfall of laughter that starts coming out of me. Of course, I'm laughing *at* everyone, which is terribly rude, and the only thing I can think to do to cover it up is to start jumping up and down and dancing. I could run out of the room, but as the expression goes, when life gives you lemons, make lemonade—or in this case when life gives you bananas, make HappyWow.

Soon I'm full-out dancing. The whole thing is so ridiculous that I'm laughing so hard I'm having trouble catching my breath. An hour ago I was with one of the theater's most important directors, and now I am a dancing happy banana in front of the creator of HappyWow.

Mr. Fukishima screams a few rapid words, and the interpreter yells out over all the commotion, "Pride. Pride. Don't forget. You are proud bananas." This note does little to change the behavior of any of the girls, including myself. We all keep dancing and laughing.

I look around at the other girls and suddenly realize they don't feel self-conscious at all. They're just dancing around, having a good time. I'm so exhausted from laughing and dancing that my resistance to the whole situation collapses. I keep laughing and jumping, but for the first time I'm just one of the other bananas, and for a few seconds I don't feel silly at all.

"Tang. Tang. Happy. Clang. Clang. Wow. Tang. Clang. Happy wow. Happy wow. HappyWOW! Tang. Taaaang."

CHAPTER 28

As I leave the studio and make my way back to the elevators, I'm still giggling, thinking about what happened. I think, if only there was a camera there to capture all of it, but of course there was a camera there, so the entire thing has been preserved for eternity. This makes me laugh harder as I press the button for the elevator. The doors opens and I am face-to-face with Chuck.

"Oh, so you were laughing at me before I even showed up," he says as he walks out of the elevator. I look at him, dressed head to toe in his lime-green tie-dyed T-shirt and the green paisley pants from Rafi's, and I can't help but laugh. It's not that he looks bad; he doesn't. In fact, he looks like he's the lead singer for some band. What makes me laugh is that you can easily tell how uncomfortable he is.

"I'm not laughing at you," I tell him so as not

to make him even more uncomfortable. "I mean, I wasn't. I just finished my audition, and it was one of the strangest experiences I've ever had in my life." I explain how silly we all looked and the interpreter and the screaming. He laughs.

"But don't worry. Mr. Fukishima was only there for the bananas. The other fruits are all going in as a bunch in the studio on the other side."

"That's good. I'm not sure I know how to be a proud banana."

"Well, neither did I. In fact, I've never been so sure that I didn't do well at an audition in my entire life. Hey, how was the movie last night? What did you see, anyway?" I ask.

"We saw *Ninja Lunchroom*. First screening, opening night. It was awesome."

I've seen a few billboards for this movie around town, and it looks like one of the stupidest things I have ever heard of. The image on the poster is a school lunch tray with an apple, a sandwich, and then a nunchak or some other ninja weapon where you would expect to see a carton of milk or some applesauce. I've a read a few reviews of the movie by respected critics who said it was awful. I mean, that might be the type of movie I would go see on a rainy day when there was absolutely nothing else available, but I'm not going to run out and see it the first weekend it opens.

"It was awesome?" My voice goes up at the end, expressing my doubt. "Really?"

"Oh yeah," he says. The other elevator opens, and more runaways from the rainbow enter the lobby and make their way to their audition. "I'm gonna see it again in, like, two weeks when the crowds aren't as huge. You should come."

"To *Ninja Lunchroom*? Are you serious? Chuck, I'm sure it's just a bunch of kids pretending to throw karate chops at each other during a food fight where a—" I try to think if the stupidest plot point I can imagine—"a bowl of Jell-O lands on the principal's head."

"Hey, I thought you said you didn't see it. How did you know that?"

I can't tell if he's being serious. Then I suddenly remember that Preston asked me out to watch the Seggermans at his mother's in two weeks. It's not like the two events conflict with each other time-wise, but when I put the two of them in my mind, they conflict on a much deeper level.

I look at Chuck for a second with a more critical eye. Yes, he has been very nice to me and he is extremely cute, but could there ever really be anything between us? I mean, maybe we could be friends, but I wonder. He likes basketball and silly movies. I like the theater and independent film. We really don't have anything in common. Besides, Preston has already asked me out on a date, so it's not like I can start going out with every guy who might show interest.

"I don't want you to get stuck behind a long line of cherries and grapes," I say, and notice that the elevator doors are opening again. I run toward them and say, "I'll see you around, Chuck. Bye."

I hop into the elevator as the doors are about to close.

Preston takes acting as seriously as I do. I think about how polished and professional he is, and while it isn't a criteria for crushing on someone, the fact that he comes from a very prestigious family doesn't hurt. The elevator doors open in the lobby, and as I exit, a whole new bunch of bananas about my age make their way into the elevator.

The passing fruit suddenly makes me remember that Preston's prestigious family is as much of an obstacle as it is an attraction.

CHAPTER 29

"Isabel, querida! Hurry up, we are going to be late," my dad yells from the living room.

"I'm almost ready," I yell back, and quickly put on the small white pearl earrings that I always wear to church. Chernique is a soloist in the choir today, so I'm super excited to go to the service, even if it means I have to sit in the pew without her. It's an incredible honor to be a soloist, but it means she has to get up at the crack of dawn in order to go over the music for the service.

My parents and I meet Chernique's mom on the corner of Essex and Stanton Streets. The adults all talk as we walk, and I just sort of follow behind them, because I'm still half-asleep.

We go to an interdenominational church off Christopher Street in the West Village. It's more like a party than what most people think of as a church, and there are literally people from every corner of the world in the congregation. The woman who runs the service was born in Kenya, the man who directs the music is French and actually wears a beret, and the woman who organizes the youth group is from the Philippines. My mom always says that we're like a mini United Nations. Whenever we have a covered dish for a church social, the table is always spread with the most unusual and delicious foods you could imagine.

As we enter the church, the choir is singing "Amazing Grace." But it's not the version you usually hear. The tempo is upbeat and full of energy, and as people enter the space, they join in with the singing and start clapping. I see Chernique onstage in the front row of the choir. Her royal-blue choir robe sways from side to side in time to the music. She eyes me, and I give her a small wave. She winks but keeps singing.

In the middle of the service the choir sings "Under the Milky Way." It's a song about how we're all connected through the same spirit. It's not what you would call a religious song, but it definitely feels spiritual, and Chernique's solo is breathtaking. Her voice has a clarity to it and this full, rich tone that fills the church. When she belts the high notes, they go right through you. If she weren't my best friend, I might be jealous of her. Music comes so naturally to her. She opens her mouth and out comes the most beautiful art. I feel like I have to work so hard to create the smallest moment of beauty.

After the service, we all wait for Chernique on the steps of the church. It takes her some extra time to finish up with the choir director and change out of her robe. When she comes out my dad is the first to congratulate her, "Chernique, *querida*, your voice is the reason half those people are in that church."

"Now, Manuel, that is almost blasphemy," Chernique's mom says. "You be careful—we're standing on the Lord's steps right now." Chernique's mom is always teasing my dad.

"Suzanne, you know I don't mean any disrespect, but just to show my heart is in the right place, why don't I buy us all brunch at the Lafayette?"

"Now that sounds like a deal," Chernique's mom says. The adults walk ahead of us as Chernique and I follow behind.

"You know, my dad is right," I tell her. "You do have an amazing voice."

"You're my best friend. You have to say that," she says.

"Well, I might have to say it, but I don't have to mean it, and I do mean it." I lock my arm around hers, and we follow our parents to the restaurant.

Since it's Sunday afternoon, the Lafayette is packed. There are only booths and small café tables in the restaurant, and it's too crowded for everyone to sit together. Instead our parents take a booth, and Chernique and I take a small table for two right next to them. Chernique and I have no problem with this, since it will allow us to talk privately.

"So, I have some good news and some bad news," I tell her.

"What's the bad news? Let's get it out of the way," she says as she nervously plays with her silverware.

"I was not a very proud banana," I say.

"Excuse me?" she asks, cocking her head to the side. But before I can explain, Bernadette, a waitress at the Lafayette who has probably taken our order a hundred times, comes over. Chernique gets the chicken salad and I order the cheeseburger deluxe, extra-crispy fries.

While we're waiting for our food, I tell Chernique

the whole terrible story, and she laughs at all the right parts. I tell her about the sea of yellow girls and the kids in the other fruit colors and about the interpreter and the crazy Japanese director. When I'm at the end of the story I repeat what the director said: "You are not just happy bananas but also proud. PROUD BANANAS!"

When Bernadette brings us our food, she says, "Banana smoothie?"

Chernique and I lose it and erupt in a fit of laughter. Of course, Bernadette has no idea why we're laughing so hard. "Something I said?"

"No," I say. "We're sorry for laughing. You have incredible timing."

By the time Bernadette puts down the last plate, we are still giggling.

"It was pretty random," I say, but then decide to explain why this is bad news. "The thing is, this was a huge commercial that would never have been seen in this country. It was my one shot at earning enough money for the academy and remaining under the Banner radar."

"I tell you, that Patricia Banner is getting on my last nerve. You have to do what you have to do. Who cares what she thinks?"

"I do," I say quickly. "I have a scholarship with her name on it."

Chernique takes a bite out of her chicken salad sandwich, and I make sure our parents are deeply involved in their conversation before I start telling her my good news.

"Are you ready for my good news?"

"Sure," she says with an eager smile on her face.

"Guess who has a date?"

Her eyes grow ten times in size, and she puts down her chicken sandwich. "You know, if our parents weren't, like, five feet from us right now, I would scream at the top of my lungs."

"I'm fully aware of that."

"I can't believe he asked you out. I mean, I could tell he liked you and everything from the way you talked about him, but . . . wow. So where is Chuck taking you?"

"Chuck?" I say, wrinkling my face. "Not Chuck. Preston. Preston asked me *on a date* to watch the Seggerman Awards at his house. Not Chuck," I repeat. "Preston."

"Oh," she says, and chews on a few chips from the side of her plate.

"Is that all you have to say, 'oh'? Chernique, I

know you have an opinion about everything, so you better just tell me now."

"It's that whenever you talk about Chuck, he seems like a cool guy and it seems easy for you to hang out with him."

"So? What does that have to do with Preston?"

"C'mon, Isabel. Don't you think Preston is a bit of a, you know, snob?"

"No," I say, just to get it out there. "I think he's serious about acting, and he has high standards." I thought Chernique would be excited for me. I count on her opinion for so much, but this time she's wrong. Isn't she? "Look, we don't want people to judge us because we aren't rich, so we shouldn't judge other people because they are."

She finally nods her head in agreement. "I guess so. It's just that whenever you talk about Preston, you're terrified he and his family are going to find out about you being a dancing banana or something."

"Well, I told you, I totally blew that audition, so there's no need to worry about that anymore. Honey is never going to call me again."

Suddenly my phone vibrates in my pocket.

Usually my calls are from Chernique or my parents. I hit the decline button without looking at the number and put the phone back in my pocket, but as soon as I put it there, it vibrates again.

"You better get that," Chernique says. "It could be important."

I grab my phone and head out to the street. The phone is still ringing when I get outside. I put it up to my face and say, "Hello."

"Hello," the voice on the other end says. "Have I got incredible news for you. . . ."

CHAPTER 30

I guess I spoke too soon about blowing my audition and never hearing from Honey again. I had to dig my yellow pants out of the trash. After my audition, I was sure there was little chance of me ever needing them again, but when Honey called me during brunch on Sunday to tell me I actually got a callback, I went through the trash to find them. Luckily, they were not underneath a bunch of actual rotten bananas.

I was shocked that I actually got a callback. I didn't think I was a particularly proud or happy banana. But when Honey told me what she thought this commercial might pay, I actually dropped my cell phone. Luckily, I was sitting on a bench outside the Lafayette, so it landed in my lap.

So once again, I'm dressed head to toe in yellow,

and I'm headed to the casting studio to be the best banana I can be for the callback.

The elevator doors open, and it's not nearly the circus it was at the initial audition. I see from the chalkboard outside the elevator that HappyWow is in studio D, so I walk down the hall to the other side of the building. There are only a handful of girls outside the studio, but everyone is wearing yellow again. The same woman is standing behind the sign-in table, but she looks much calmer than she did the other day.

I know I need to pick up my size card from the audition the other day, but when I reach the table, the woman behind it says, "Hi, 217. I have you right over here?"

"Excuse me?" I say. I think this woman just called me a number.

"You are 217, right?" she asks, and then picks up a card from the other side of the table and holds it up to me. Stapled to the card is a Polaroid of me from the other day, wearing the exact same thing I am wearing right now and holding a piece of paper with the number 217 on it.

"Yes," I say. "That's me. My name is Isabel."

"That's right, 217," she says, like I'm the crazy one for trying to use my real name. "Mr. Fukishima is going very fast. You'll be called in soon."

"Thanks," I say, and take my card and sit on one of the folding chairs outside the studio.

"Isabel, I think you're the only person here who doesn't look like they drank a bad can of HappyWow. You actually look good in yellow," a voice next to me says.

"Brittany, how are you?" I ask.

"How do you think I am? I'm here for a callback for a commercial that no one will ever see, and I look awful in yellow. Everyone does, except you. Look at these other girls." She gestures to the three or four other girls sitting right next to us and makes a face of disgust. The girls who have been sitting there silently look at each other with a bit of disbelief like, did she just do that? Of course, some of them have known Brittany for years, so they know the answer to the question is definitely yes.

"Anyway," Brittany continues, "this commercial is only going to air in Japan, so what's the point?"

"My agent said it pays a lot of money," I tell her.

"Oh, I'm sure it pays a ton, but it's like if a tree

falls in a forest and there's no one there to hear it, does it still make a sound? In my book, it's like the tree never fell in the first place but . . . Oh, I just remembered. You know how I told you my dad has a client who's a producer of that new musical, *Super Claw*? Well, they gave my dad a box. We have extra tickets. Do want to go with us this weekend?"

"That would be amazing, Brit. I love Broadway and I hardly ever get to go. Are you sure it's okay? What about Phoebe?" I ask. I would never want to come between two friends.

"Phoebe and Cassie hate comic books, and if they want to come too, they can. We've got plenty of seats. So?" she asks while nudging me with her elbow. "Are you gonna ask that cute boy you like?"

For a second Chuck's face pops into my head when she asks me this question. I bet he would love *Super Claw*. I don't really know if he likes comic books, but my hunch is he does. However, I realize Brittany is asking me about Preston. Preston is really the boy I'm interested in. He's already asked me out. I can't imagine Preston loving a show like *Super Claw*, but it is Broadway. Who could turn down an invitation to Broadway?

"I guess I could ask Preston," I tell her.

"Great! I'll e-mail you all the details. We're driving in from Long Island, and my dad can pick you up or something."

The door to the studio opens, and the woman with the clipboard says, "217, please."

"That's me," I say.

"Break a leg, 217!"

Inside the studio I recognize the casting people, Mr. Fukishima, and the interpreter, Miko. Behind the camera there are about half a dozen Japanese businessmen, all in blue suits, all wearing glasses. When I walk in front of the camera, everyone sort of bows toward me, so I bow back, assuming that's the polite thing to do. The woman with the clipboard says, "This is Isabel Marak Flores."

It's the first time anyone connected with HappyWow has actually called me by my name, and it feels a bit like being human again—and just when I'm supposed to be a potassium-rich fruit. Once again, Mr. Fukishima yells something in Japanese, but this time some of the men in business suits join in the yelling. Then the interpreter, Miko, tells me to go through the same routine.

The same boy from the other day with the

brightly colored hair starts the music. This time I'm prepared for it.

"*Tang. Tang. Happy. Clang. Clang. Wow. Tang. Clang. Happy wow. Happy wow. HappyWOW! Tang. Taaaang.*"

I'm a happy banana but also one with great pride. With every bounce and jump I make during the callback, I think of all the money I could earn if I land this spot. I think about attending the academy next year and walking through the halls that so many great actors have walked through, and that thought makes me truly happy and proud.

CHAPTER 31

Super Claw is the most talked-about Broadway musical since, well, ever. It's everywhere. You can't walk down the street without seeing a billboard for it or turn on the radio without hearing a news story about how someone has been injured during one of the super-intense action scenes. The whole show is based on the very popular comic books, which were then turned into blockbuster movies and are now coming to life on Broadway.

I call Preston, pretending that I have a question about our scene from *Romeo and Juliet*. I didn't want to call him up and only ask if he wanted to go see this show. That would have been much too forward. As we're wrapping up and saying good-bye, I just sort of mention the show as if it was the most natural thing in the world.

"Guess I'll see you at rehearsal," I say. "Oh,

wait. A bunch of my friends have tickets to see *Super Claw* this weekend. Do you want to go?"

"*Super Claw*? Are you serious?" he asks with a bit of condescension in his voice. Oh, why couldn't Brittany's dad work with the guy producing *Our Town*?

"Yeah, I know it's not exactly Shakespeare, but my friend has free tickets and . . ." I try to keep my tone upbeat and casual.

"Sure," he finally says. "Why not?"

"Oh, all right," I say, and tell him I'll e-mail him about it later. Phew.

As soon as I get off the phone, I wonder if I made a mistake inviting Preston. While his less-than-enthusiastic response to *Super Claw* was not a great sign, I didn't realize until after I invited him that I would have to explain how I know Brittany. I can't very well tell him that we hang out every now and then, hoping to play different types of fruits for various different countries. Luckily, no one likes a plan more than Brittany, so when I explain the situation to her, I'm sure she'll be more than happy to keep Preston in the dark about how we know each other.

• • •

A few minutes before Brittany and her family are scheduled to pick me up, I take one last look in the mirror. I'm wearing a very elegant black velvet dress with little crystal accents near the collar and on the cuffs of the sleeves. It's perfect for a night on Broadway, because it's simple and black, but the crystals add a touch of style.

I hear the elevator door of the apartment open, and I quickly head to the living room. We're meeting Preston there since he lives so close to the theater district, so it's just Brittany's family at the door. I show Brit, her sister Christine, and Liam around the apartment while our parents get to know each other. As soon as we're alone and out of the living room, Brittany turns to me and says, "Did you hear anything about the HappyWow spot?"

"Uh-oh," Liam says. "Looks like we picked up the wrong Brittany tonight. We got the old Brittany." He pretends to knock on her forehead and says, "What did you do with my girlfriend? Is the girl who loves to draw and doesn't take commercials too seriously in there? Hellooooo?"

Liam is teasing, but it's clear Brittany is not amused. "For your information, I'm not asking for me. I'm asking for Isabel."

"Sure you are," Christine says, and gives Brittany a look.

"Look, I don't even want to book the spot. It airs in Japan, and I could care less if my face is seen on the other side of the world."

"She's got a point," Christine says. "Asia is not her favorite continent."

"Thank you, Christine," she says, and then turns to Liam. "I'm asking because this could be a huge spot for her, and Judith says they may be letting people know tonight because it shoots next week."

"Who's Judith?" I ask.

"My agent since I was in diapers," Brittany says like it's the most normal thing in the world to have had an agent since you were in diapers. "Judith said that they're really pressed for time, so they're making calls tonight."

"Tonight? But it's Friday night and we'll be at the show," I say.

"Just put your phone on vibrate."

Honestly, I wasn't even thinking of bringing my phone, since it's totally forbidden to get a call during a performance, but I guess I could check it during intermission.

"C'mon, kids. We don't want to be late," I hear Brittany's mom yell from the living room. I open the door to my bedroom to head back out, but Brittany stops me before I can open it all the way.

"Now everyone, remember: No one says anything about anything related to commercials. We don't want to blow it for Isabel in front of Preston." She makes her way out of my bedroom.

"Wait. Wait!" Liam shrieks like he's seen a ghost or something. "Does anyone have a voice recorder or something? Say that again, Brit. Please. I want to record it."

Brittany just keeps on walking, rolls her eyes, and says to me, "Lucky me. I have a boyfriend who is not only great at drawing but also thinks he's a comedian."

When we arrive at the theater, Preston is already in front, waiting for us. I introduce him to everyone, and of course Brittany's parents find him utterly charming because he's so well mannered, and there's that British accent. They tell me so as we make our way through the line to enter the theater. I'm not surprised. Preston is the type of boy parents always like.

Mr. Rush gives our tickets to the usher, and as

I walk past the usher, I can't help but feel a rush of excitement. There is nothing like the theater, and Broadway is a very special place. Every Broadway theater has its own charm, but the Skyway Airlines Theater is brand-new, and every detail is streamlined and refined. Instead of gold-leaf cherubs adorning the lobby, there are highly polished slabs of pink and gray marble. Everyone is chattering as we enter, but I'm silent. I know I'm in a place that is special, and I just want to take everything in, from the sound of the ushers guiding people to their seats to the smell of the freshly printed Playbills.

We walk up the stage-left staircase to our seats. The box is on the side of the theater but big enough so we have a perfect view of the stage, and Brittany's parents can be on one side while the kids can be on the other. The box also gives us a fantastic view of the audience. I look down at everyone waiting in anticipation for the show to start.

I can't wait until I make my Broadway debut. I know a small part of it has to do with luck, but I believe you can make your own luck. The other the part is hard work. I have complete control over how hard I work, and I have every intention of making my dreams come true.

"These seats are great. I can't wait for it to start!" Liam says.

"You'll excuse my boyfriend's enthusiasm. He is obsessed with comic books."

"So are you!" Liam says, and he gives Brittany a look. It's the kind of look where you can tell he likes her. The two of them bicker a lot, but you know they totally dig each other. They have this chemistry, and sometimes it overflows a bit.

"I'm obsessed with manga, which is a type of comic book. *Super Claw* is all right, but not my first choice," Brittany says.

Liam looks at the stage and then at the back of the theater, like he's trying to figure something out. "I bet his claw will totally fly over our heads when he attacks the Nappert. Brit, you better be ready to duck."

"Over our heads?" Preston asks. "You mean, he's going to leave the stage? Is this in the round?"

"The round? I dunno, but the best part is when his claw comes out and chases the bad guy, who's supposed to fly over the audience." Liam is unable to hide his excitement.

Preston scowls and then whispers in my ear, "Goodness. Not exactly Shakespeare, is it?"

I smile a little at Preston when he says this, and just then the lights begin to dim. I think it's sort of rude of him to make fun of the play when it was so nice of Brittany to invite us. Luckily, I don't have to think about this too much, because the orchestra has begun playing and the magic of the theater is starting.

CHAPTER 32

Act one of Super Claw ends with one of the most amazing things I have ever seen. Super Claw is battling the evil Nappert, a computer that went rogue and is trying to destroy mankind. Everyone in the cast is singing the most upbeat and frenetic song from the show, "Do or Die," and just as you think Super Claw is about to get Nappert, Nappert transforms into a 3-D hologram that suddenly bounces around the theater, and then there's an explosion onstage, and through a puff of smoke you see a 3-D hologram of Super Claw. It crosses back and forth across the stage as the chorus sings, "Do or die, don't you cry. Do or . . ." As they are about to sing the last note of the song, there is another explosion, only this time it happens in the middle of the audience, above everyone's head. People in the audience shriek out of either fear or excitement, or both. There was so much going on, I'm not sure I understood it all, but it was certainly breathtaking.

The lights slowly come up for intermission, and I think about what must be going on backstage, how the actors are changing costumes and the stage crew is probably clearing the stage. For a second, I long to be backstage and not in the audience. I yearn for the excitement of being behind the scenes.

"That. Was. Amazing," Liam says, his eyes still fixed on the spot above the audience where the explosion took place.

"I really like the scene where the Nappert flew down that zipline," Christine says.

"I thought the costumes were perfect. In fact, the one Super Claw's girlfriend was wearing gave me an idea for a drawing I might try this weekend," Brittany says.

"The two of them carry their sketch pads everywhere," Christine says to Preston and me.

"Please," Brittany says, interrupting. "The only way we got Christine to leave her soccer ball at home was to have my dad tell her we didn't get a ticket for it. But what do you guys think of the show?"

I look at Preston, and I can tell by his face that he isn't enjoying it nearly as much as I am. "I thought the singing was excellent. It must be very hard to sing while tumbling through the air," I say, smiling. I'm surprised I liked the first act as much as I did.

"And Preston." Brittany nudges him. "What do you think?"

Preston looks down at the ground for a second and then says, "Well, you know, I was raised in the theater. My first show in the West End was seeing my mother in a Beckett play."

"Ohhh!" Christine squeals. "We had a rabbit named Beckett when we were little."

"You had a rabbit named after the famous playwright Samuel Beckett?"

"Who?" Christine asks. "Samuel Beckett? No. We named him after a character on a cartoon we watched."

"Of course you did," Preston says with a sneer. "Isabel, why don't we go and get some air?" He gets up and walks past Brittany and everyone else without even looking at them.

I don't know what to say. I just get up and follow him out of the box. "We'll be outside if you want to come along," I say, hoping that will be enough to smooth things over.

We find a corner outside the theater on the street, away from anyone who is smoking. An actor has to be careful of any secondhand smoke, as it can damage the voice. Once we find an adequate location, Preston says, "Oh, this is the most dreadful thing I've seen since I saw Cyndi Lauper in *Medea*. It's that awful. Oh, Isabel, you are such a good friend to pretend that you like it in front of your friends. I really admire you."

The truth is, I wasn't pretending at all. I'm not sure it's my favorite musical in the world, but I'm certainly enjoying it. "It's not that bad," I say.

Preston laughs out loud. "Oh, Isabel, we're alone. You don't have to pretend with me. There isn't a shred of artistic value in this whatsoever. I can't wait to get home and tell my mum about what a mess this whole production is. When I tell her that the chorus actually sings while doing somer-saults, she'll laugh out loud. I can just hear it. She'll really get a kick out of declaring the end of the theater as we know it."

Before I can come up with a response, I see Brittany running out of the theater and over to us.

"Hey, guys. I wanted to run to the ladies' room before the second act."

"You ran out here to tell us that?" Preston asks.

"Well, you know how girls always like to do this sort of thing in pairs," she says, then grabs me by the arm and takes me back inside. "See you at our seats, Prest."

Once we're in the lobby, she lets go of my arm and I say, "What's going on? Do you feel all right?"

"Oh, I feel fine. I only said that to get you alone. Boys will believe anything. Did you check your texts?" she asks.

"No," I tell her. I had my phone totally off during the show, of course.

"C'mon over to the back corner of the lobby," she says. "That's where I got a signal." She walks to an area away from the door, near the emergency exit.

"Why would I want to check . . ." I start to say, and then I remember. "Oh! Did you book HappyWow?"

"No," she says, "but I just got a text message from my agent saying I was released, so that means they've made their final decisions. Check your phone."

I open my purse, pull out my small, shiny phone, and turn it on. Brit and I are both staring at the thing like it's a crystal ball, and in a way it is. When the screen finally illuminates we both see it: NEW TEXT MESSAGE. FROM: HONEY ARBUCKLE. I hit enter and read the message:

CONGRATULATIONS! YOU BOOKED HAPPYWOW. CALL ME TOMORROW FOR ALL THE DETAILS. SHOOTS ON TUESDAY. YOU'LL BE HUGE IN JAPAN."

"That's great!" Brittany shouts. "That's really great."

I'm still in such shock that I can't actually make words yet. Booking this spot means I will actually be able to attend the academy, and no one will ever find out how I was able to pay for it. I can't believe it. I'm about to let my joy register, but then I remember that because I booked it, that means Brittany didn't. "Oh, Brittany, I'm sorry you didn't . . ."

She doesn't let me finish. "Oh, please. I've already been in enough commercials to fill a film festival, and like I told you, I don't give a flip about being seen in another country. Do you realize how big a spot this is?" It's clear she is much more excited for me than she is disappointed for herself.

"No, I don't think I do."

"Well, it's *huge*."

Just then the chimes indicating the start of act two sound, so we start walking toward our seats.

"Remember," I tell Brittany. "Not a word of this to Preston."

"I promise. Not talking to Preston won't be a problem," Brittany says, and rolls her eyes.

CHAPTER 33

Four days later a car is waiting to take my dad and me to the set of the HappyWow commercial. My parents spoke with Honey on the phone, and they only agreed to let me miss a day of school if one of them was on the set for the day. Honey said that a minor had to have either an official guardian on set, provided by the production company, or a parent. Since I've never actually booked a commercial before, Honey suggested that at least one of my parents go with me. My mom teaches on Tuesdays, and my dad was able to do some of his work for his upcoming show on his laptop, so he's the one coming with me.

We get into the backseat of the town car hired by the makers of HappyWow to whisk us from our apartment on the Lower East Side to a production studio in Queens. We could get to the studio in about the same amount of time by taking the subway, but they insisted on sending a car, because we have to be at the studio by five o'clock a.m. for a full day of shooting.

"Are you nervous, *mija*?" my dad asks as I stare out the window, watching the city streets slowly wake up as sunlight peeks through the morning clouds.

"No," I say. "Not really. I mean, it's just for TV. It's not like there will even be an audience there, and I don't say anything except, 'HappyWow.' I can't believe it's going to take all day."

Since the streets are almost empty, we get from our apartment, over the bridge, and to the studio in almost no time. The driver opens the door for us, and we head into the reception area. As soon as we walk in, a woman with her hair in a high ponytail, wearing a Yankees jersey and holding a clipboard, comes over. "You must be Isabel," she says. "I'm Pam, the PA assigned to you today. Is this your dad?"

"Yes," I say, as my dad shakes hands with Pam and explains that this is our first commercial booking.

"Well," Pam says, "don't worry about a thing. I'll show you to your dressing room, and then we'll go over the schedule. If you or your dad need anything, anything at all today, let me know."

"That's great," I say. "Thank you."

Pam leads us down a long hall and opens the thick, heavy doors to the set that keep noise out while they're filming. "That's the set you'll be filming on, and the dressing rooms and all the wardrobe and catering are on the other side."

"That's the set?" I ask.

"Yeah, isn't it great?" Pam says as she keeps walking along the edge of the massive studio toward the dressing rooms.

The set is unlike any set I have ever seen in the theater. Usually the set tries to re-create a place like a library or someone's bedroom. This is entirely green. It's bright lime green, like the kind that would give you a headache if you looked at it for too long. There is a green background and a green floor and then some strange shapes like rectangles and squares with wheels that are also green. I don't understand what it's supposed to be, but I have the feeling I won't totally understand a lot of what happens today.

We get to the dressing room I'll be using for the day, and it has my name on a piece of masking tape on the door. Pam opens the door and says, "Sorry, the dressing rooms in this studio are super small."

"It's great," I say, and think about the dressing rooms backstage in the theater, where space is at a premium. This one is absolutely palatial compared to those.

"Well, don't worry, because you won't be spending much time in here today. You have a very busy schedule," she says, and places the schedule down on the makeup table in front of me. "But don't worry, Mr. Flores. I'll make sure we adhere to the union contract and take the necessary breaks, and if she needs a break to do homework, we'll make sure that happens as well."

"Thank you, Pam. It looks like she is in good hands."

Pam looks at her watch and says, "Well, I've got to get you to wardrobe for your fitting." I look down at the schedule and see that wardrobe is the first thing on the list, but they have two whole hours blocked out for it. How long can it actually take? "Do you want to come with us or stay here, Mr. Flores?"

"I know you have the gallery blueprint to go over, Dad. I'm fine. You stay here."

"Are you sure?" he asks.

"Yep," I say, and Pam and I head to wardrobe.

I expect to find a sewing machine and a plump lady with a measuring tape draped around her neck, but when Pam opens the door marked WARDROBE, I feel like I've entered the inside of a computer. At first I think we're in the wrong room, since I don't see any banana costumes.

"This is Isabel," Pam says.

"I'm Mark," says a guy with glasses, a goatee, and a T-shirt with the symbol for NASA on it. "I'm in charge of wardrobe, and I have yours right over here." He reaches for a small shopping bag that looks like it could barely fit a real banana, let alone a banana costume. Yet when he hands it to me, I notice the tag on it says BANANA GIRL, so it must be mine. At least Banana Girl is better than being called by a number. "You can change over there," he says, and points to an area behind a curtain.

Then I realize that my costume must be waiting for me behind the curtain. I go to the changing area and close the curtain behind me, but I don't see anything. Nothing. I think about going back to Mark and asking him where my costume is, but instead I shout from behind the curtain. I'm sure they'll realize the mistake quickly and send Pam back with it. "Excuse me," I say. "I'm sorry, but I don't see my costume back here."

"What?" Mark shouts back, because he's on the other side of the room.

"My costume? I don't see it."

"It's in the bag," he says.

At first I think I didn't hear him correctly, but what else could he have said? I take the small bag from the chair I set it on and look in it.

Green. Lime, eye-hurting green.

I put my hand into the bag and pull out something in the shape of the hood of a jacket, but it's made of green spandex. I pull out the other two pieces, and clearly one is a pair of spandex leggings and the other is a long-sleeved spandex top, all in the exact same shade of green.

"Everything okay back there?" Pam asks from the other side of the curtain.

"Fine," I say. "Everything is fine." Of course, everything is *not* fine. It's far from fine. I don't care if this commercial is only going to be seen in Japan.

I can't be in it looking like I jumped into a lime-green balloon. Maybe something is wrong. "Um, why is the banana costume so green?" I ask. "Is this an unripe banana?"

"No, that's the performance-capture bodysuit for the CGI. You put it all on, and the hood should leave an opening for your head. The banana part and everything will be done on a computer later. I have to set it up so the sensors on your suit match up with the computer sensors. Are you almost ready?"

"Just a minute," I yell back. I have no idea what a performance-capture bodysuit is, but I have a hunch it's not going to be a good look for me. I put on the garments as quickly as I can, but it takes a few minutes to figure out what is an armhole and what is the hood for my head. When I finish, I turn to look at myself in the mirror, but the second I see my image I scream, "Ahhh!"

"Is everything all right?" Pam asks.

"Yes," I say. Again, I am totally lying. I can't look at myself in the mirror. I am completely covered in green spandex, including most of my head—except for my face, which pops out like someone is pushing my head through a drinking straw. I never thought I would actually be in a position to wish that I was wearing a banana costume, but right now I would trade anything for some yellow foam. I take a deep breath and head out of the dressing room.

CHAPTER 34

Once Mark is finished connecting the sensors, I'm allowed to walk back to my dressing room. As soon as the door opens, my father sees me and breaks out in hysterical laughter. I just stand there in my spandex and wait for him to stop.

"Dad, I want to make sure you know that, as my parent and official guardian, your job is to *support* me."

"Of course, *mija.* I love you, but you do look a little . . . funny," he says with a sheepish grin.

"A little?" I ask. "A *little* funny? I look like I'm about to be sent into space."

"But why green? You are a banana, not a *plátano,* right?"

"Yes, Dad. I don't think they have *plátanos* in Japan." I force myself to look in the mirror in the dressing room. He's right. I look more like the green starchy banana-shaped fruit he grew up eating in El Salvador than I do a banana. I explain to him that all the graphics are going to be placed on me using some computer program.

Someone knocks on the door. My dad opens it and Pam says, "They're ready for you on set. Mr. Flores, you can watch on the monitor in here." She turns on the small TV. The bright-green set suddenly appears on the screen, and you can hear the people walking around on set. "Or you can watch on the soundstage."

"Dad, you should wait here," I say. "I don't want your laughter drowning out the sound and making us go a second longer than we have to."

"If you say so," he says, and sits back down in the chair next to the monitor.

I follow Pam to the set, and we pass by a bunch of the crew. No one looks at me funny, so that makes me feel a little better. Still, it's weird to show up and have the set done and the costume created. When I'm in a play, it's all about building a community. During the rehearsals, I get to know people and make friends. Except for Pam and Mark, I don't think I know another person's name.

When we get to the set, I recognize Mr.

Fukishima and his interpreter, Miko. I assume I'm going to be officially introduced to them, but Pam tells me to go directly to the center of the sound-stage, where the green set is so brightly lit that my eyes tear and I squint for a few seconds before they adjust to the light. "Stand on your mark," Pam says. "The blue X on the floor made with tape." We use the same thing in the theater, so I know where to go. I stand on my mark and wait.

It's just like the audition and the callback. Mr. Fukishima yells something and then the interpreter talks to me. First she says, "Can we hear your lines?" My one line in the commercial is, "HappyWow!" Honey faxed over a page with this line on Monday, and it took me all of one second to memorize. I say the line out loud, and every single Japanese person in the room, and there are a lot, starts laughing. Then everyone else starts laughing. They can't be laughing at my costume, because frankly you can't tell where my costume begins and the set ends.

Miko says, "Very, very good. You say it so funny."

"Thank you," I say, not sure what I should say. I can't imagine I say it any differently from any other girl, but I got the booking, so there you go.

Mr. Fukishima yells in Japanese and then gives a countdown, again in Japanese. When he gets to the end of his countdown, the speakers in the studio crackle and then, streaming out of them, I hear:

"Tang. Tang. Happy. Clang. Clang. Wow. Tang. Clang. Happy wow. Happy wow. HappyWOW! Tang. Taaaang."

It's the same "music" from the audition. I thought I had erased it from my memory forever, but once I hear it again, I know it will be with me forever, like some type of audio tattoo.

For the rest of the day Mr. Fukishima screams, Miko translates, and then I perform every possible ridiculous pose, dance, and gesture there is in the world, all the while telling myself that it'll all be worth it when I'm at the academy next year. All the other fruits are sitting on magic "wheelbarrows" (the interpreter couldn't think of the proper word, so they're not really wheelbarrows, they're like enormous mushrooms with an escape hatch and wheels, but close enough) and I dance around visiting them. None of the other kids playing the other fruits are actually there, because they plan to shoot them later and use the computer to splice it all together. The computer can only handle one live performer at a time. At each magic "wheelbarrow" I say my line and then do a different happy dance that also, of course, contains pride.

Six hours later I feel like I have heard the Happy Wow jingle at least six thousand times. It is burned into my brain. I know I won't be able to erase it from my memory, because I begin to feel like the jingle *is* my memory, like someone has taken out my brain and implanted a chip that plays it on a loop. Even when Mr. Fukishima yells, "Cut!" one of the only three English words he seems to know, the other two being "coffee" and, of course, "banana," I still hear the "music" in my head. I wonder if I'll have to take some type of medication to have it removed.

Mr. Fukishima insists we do one last take. I'm at that point in the day where I am just acting silly, so on the last take I let go and act like a complete and total moron. I talk to the other fruits and make silly faces. I mug at the camera and smile and stick out my tongue at one point.

I had always hoped to visit Japan one day, but as the day finally finishes and Mr. Fukishima yells, "Wrap it!" followed by the interpreter saying, "I think he means, 'that's a wrap,'" I realize that I will never be able to set foot in that country for the next fifty years.

My dad helps me carry my stuff to the town car, which is waiting to drive us home, and even though I am so tired I can barely think, a wide smile moves across my face and a feeling of contentment settles in. I did it. I booked the spot that will pay for the academy, and no one in this country will ever see it.

CHAPTER 35

Two weeks later my life is perfect.

Perfect.

My parents have made arrangements with the academy to have the remainder of my tuition paid in installments. With the money from my commercial booking and the scholarship, we'll be able to afford it. I have officially enrolled for the next grading period, which starts after winter break, and told my current school that I'll be leaving. I've even made up my schedule for next semester. I'll be taking classes like Scene Study and a class in Stage Combat, something I've always wanted to do.

To add to the perfection that is my life, I'm waiting outside the theater for my final rehearsal with Preston before the benefit. I wanted to share all my good news with him about actually being able to attend the academy, but I can't, of course, because he never knew there was a chance I wouldn't be going. I guess I could tell him now, but that would mean telling him about the commercial, and that I can never do. I can't begin to imagine that the son of Patricia Banner would have anything to do with the dancing banana of the HappyWow commercial. Luckily, I don't expect the Banners to be traveling to Japan anytime soon, so HappyWow is all behind me—except for the checks that will be coming in and the very annoying fact that I still can't get the stupid jingle out of my head.

I'll be walking down the street or eating lunch at school and out of nowhere in the back of my mind I'll hear: *"Tang. Tang. Happy. Clang. Clang. Wow."* It sounds like chipmunks singing a Celine Dion song backward. You would think something so awful would leave my brain immediately, but instead it has lingered like a piece of tape on a cat's paw. I can't shake it.

"Are you ready for our final rehearsal before the big show?" Preston asks as he walks toward me outside the backstage door.

"Completely. I can't believe the benefit is next week," I say, and he reaches behind me and presses the button to let Gladys know we're downstairs.

"And don't forget," Preston says as the door buzzes and he opens it for me. "You're coming over tomorrow to watch the Seggerman Awards. My mum had the TV cable installed this weekend, and she bought a brand-new huge flat-screen TV last week, so it will feel like we're there live except for the stupid commercials."

I laugh the kind of laugh the guilty party laughs in a crime drama when someone suggests they might have committed the crime. "Yeah," I say, "those stupid commercials."

We climb the stairs to the greenroom, and as usual Gladys is sitting there, watching her little TV with the volume turned up as loud as it can go. "Hey, kids," she says, "he's almost ready for you. I'll buzz him and let him know you're here."

Then my mind starts playing tricks on me.

"Tang. Tang. Happy. Clang. Clang. Wow."

I'm hearing the HappyWow jingle in my head. I must really be losing it.

But then there's something a little different about the way it usually plays in my head. First, it's really loud, and second, it's a little staticky. Then I realize that it's not coming from inside my head. It's coming from Gladys's TV!

HappyWow is actually playing on her little TV, and I'm pretty sure her ten-inch TV doesn't pick up stations from Tokyo.

"Ahhh!" I scream. I actually scream out loud. It's not a quiet little *I forgot to feed my goldfish* gasp. It's an all-out scream.

"Are you all right?" Preston asks, and turns toward me. This gives me a split second to catch a glimpse of Gladys's TV, and sure enough, I see an extreme close-up of my face surrounded by computer-generated banana.

"What's wrong?" Gladys asks, turning away from the TV to look at me. My little screaming trick has worked. I just wanted to keep Preston away from the TV and Gladys's eyes off the screen for thirty seconds.

"Yes," I say. "I just . . . uh . . . I stubbed my toe really bad. Ahhh!" I scream again, only this time louder. They must think I'm possessed. I figure I have about ten seconds until the next commercial comes on and then I'll be safe, unless they're planning to do a HappyWow double feature.

Preston gives me quizzical look. "How did you stub your toe standing still?" he asks.

"Oh, well, that's the worst kind," I say. I never

thought I would be grateful to Fruity Pops, but when I hear the cereal commercial on the TV, I know mine is over and the coast is clear. "Look, I'm going to take care of my toe. You head into rehearsal. I'll meet you there."

Preston looks a little confused, but he heads out of the greenroom and down to the rehearsal studio. As soon as he's gone, I take out my cell phone and dial a number I thought I would never have to use again. After a few rings no one picks up, and it goes to voice mail, so I leave a message. "Hi, Honey. It's Isabel. Look, I'm having a little bit of an emergency. Can you call me as soon as you can? I have a few questions about the HappyWow commercial. Thanks."

I hang up and head to rehearsal, still in shock over the fact that HappyWow might be here in this country. The only thing I can think is *wow*, and boy, am I *not* happy.

CHAPTER 36

"But Isabel, baby, this is good news. Do you realize you're going to be famous not only in Asia but around the entire world?"

Honey says this like I have just won the lottery.

"Honey, this was only supposed to air in Japan. Small island, lots of people. Great sushi. You know, JAPAN!" I yell into the phone.

"I know, but that's how it works. You sign the contract, and you don't get to decide where it shows up. It happens. They loved the spot, and they decided to launch in the US and UK immediately. They're making a major push, sponsoring everything from sporting events to art programs. They're running print ads in all the major magazines and even making billboards!"

"Well, that's just great," I say as sarcastically as

possible, but Honey doesn't pick up on my lack of enthusiasm.

"See, that's the idea, doll," she says, and hangs up.

I turn off my cell phone and sit on my bed. Yesterday everything was perfect. A mere twenty-four hours later and everything is miserable.

"Are you ready to go?" my dad says as he knocks on my door.

"Almost, Dad," I say. "Come in."

As soon as he sees me sitting on the bed in my favorite black dress, he can tell something is wrong.

"Are you feeling all right?"

"Yeah. I mean . . . physically, I feel fine, it's just that . . ." I haven't told them that I'm about to become the laughingstock of the globe as a dancing banana.

"Well, you know that commercial I shot?"

My dad shakes his head. "Ay. I can't get that jingle out of my head. They were playing it through the monitor in your dressing room all day. Ting. Ting. Lang . . ."

"Please, stop," I say, holding up my hand. "I don't want to hear another note."

"What's going on?" he asks, sitting down on the bed next to me.

"Remember how when we left the studio, we thought we would never have to hear that song again?"

"Yes," he says. His eyebrows are furrowed in that concerned dad way.

"Well, let's just say that never isn't very far away." I explain to my dad how the makers of HappyWow liked the commercial so much that they decided to launch the product around the world, including the good old USA, and that means that I will soon be appearing as a *banana* on TV, magazines, and billboards all over the country. "Dad," I say quietly, "how can I be respected as an actor when the whole country will see me dancing around like a computer-generated idiot?"

"*Mija*, there are a lot of girls who would love to be in such a commercial."

"But the whole reason I even auditioned for the commercial was to earn enough money to pay for school."

"And you did that. Your mom and I are very proud of you. Do you know what the first painting I ever sold was?"

"No," I say.

"Well, actually it was five paintings. I had recently graduated from the fine arts school back in El Salvador. I was ready to be the next Picasso or Jackson Pollack."

"Five paintings? You must have been thrilled."

"Well, at first. The person actually commissioned me to do the paintings after seeing my work in a student show. He was a very wealthy businessman. I was excited until I found out he wanted me to paint portraits."

"Of his family?"

"Yes and no."

"I don't understand," I say.

"He wanted me to paint portraits of his five goats. He certainly considered them part of his family, and they turned out to be very nice animals, as far as goats go." Then he pauses. "Except for Chicha. She was one mean goat—she kept trying to eat the paper I sketched her on. But the other four were very nice goats, and that's how I made enough money to come to the US and meet your beautiful mother and raise our beautiful family."

I know he's telling me the story to cheer me up,

but I'm afraid it does very little to boost my spirits.

"Let's go," he says. "Grab your coat and I'll teach you how to find a goat's best side on the drive uptown." I get my coat and wonder how long I have until Preston finds out about my secret goat.

CHAPTER 37

*The Upper East Side is dominated by tall, stately build-*ings that have doormen who wait patiently to help residents with their packages or hold the leashes of their toy poodles while they chat on their cell phones (the people, not the poodles). The Banners live in a building on Fifth Avenue that overlooks the reservoir in Central Park. My dad pulls up in front of the building, and as soon as the car stops, a doorman in a tuxedo helps me out. I don't need help, but it's nice to have it around, I guess. I'm escorted into the lobby, which is decorated with fresh floral arrangements the size of a golf cart. They have branches with red and orange leaves, brightly colored yellow mums, and a bunch of gold and green flowers with pointy petals that look like pom-poms. When I tell the doorman I'm here to see the Banners, he points me toward the elevator and tells the elevator man, who is also dressed in a tuxedo, that I will be going to the thirty-third floor.

I could live in the elevator.

It's small but cozy, and elegant, not cramped. The walls are covered in finely printed powder-blue and soft-beige floral wallpaper, and there is an actual couch covered in burgundy velvet built into the walls of the elevator. There's a plush forest-green carpet that looks like a patch of finely manicured grass.

When we arrive at the top floor, I thank the elevator man and knock on the door marked PH, which I know stands for penthouse. A maid wearing an actual maid's uniform like you see in old movies opens the door and welcomes me to the Banner home. "Hors d'oeuvres are being served in the East Living Room," she says, and I follow her down the hall. Imagine having so many living rooms that you need to specify them with individual names. Our loft is almost one big open space, except for the bathroom and makeshift walls my dad built to section off the bedrooms.

The maid opens the huge double doors to the East Living Room, where the adults are chatting and sipping drinks out of glasses with long crystal stems.

I recognize a Broadway director, a theater critic for the *New York Times*, and at least two other Tony Award winners besides Preston's mother. Through the people I can see out the windows and past the terrace to a spectacular view of Central Park.

Preston sees me and starts to walk over. He looks so handsome. He's wearing a crisp pair of khaki pants, a tailored blue blazer, and a gray-and-green-plaid shirt.

"Preston," I say, tugging on his sleeve. "I thought you said your mother was inviting a few people over to watch the Seggerman Awards on TV." There are at least three dozen people here, all dressed like they're attending the awards show in person. Many of the women are wearing full-length evening gowns, and there are a few men in tuxedos. I guess they could be doormen, but I find that unlikely. "This is not a small gathering," I whisper to Preston. I don't mention the fact that this was supposed to be a date as well. It's not exactly as I imagined it.

"Well, to my mother this is a small gathering," he says. "The British ambassador was going to come, but he was called away on urgent business at the United Nations or something."

Mrs. Banner is dressed in a flowing gold lamé gown that clings to her body like she's a Greek statue. She sweeps by as Preston finishes speaking and doesn't even pretend that she wasn't eavesdropping.

"Can you believe that man?" she says. "One silly little uprising in some little country on the other side of the world and he misses my soirée."

"Mum," Preston says. "They declared a national emergency in that country."

"Oh, pish-posh. If Norma Swenson wins the award for best actress, there's going to be a national emergency right here in this apartment." She points down at the floor for emphasis as she speaks. Mrs. Banner looks behind us to the other side of the room. "Oh, do excuse me. The men from the TV company who were fixing the satellite are about to leave, and I want to make sure the reception is crystal clear. I want to be able to see the tears in Norma's eyes when she loses." Mrs. Banner runs off. For the first time since I have arrived, we are really alone, and it begins to feel like a date. Sort of.

"Are you all ready for tomorrow night?" Preston asks.

"Tomorrow night?" I ask.

"The benefit? Blimey, Isabel, you're as cool as a

cucumber. You aren't even worried about the benefit, are you? I admit I still get a little nervous. There are going to be a lot of important people there."

The truth is, I'm so preoccupied with the HappyWow situation that I haven't thought of much else. "Actually," I say, "there are a lot of important people here."

"Just my mum's chums. She actually invited James"—he pauses and corrects himself—"I mean, Mr. Tipton, but he's busy with a brand-new sponsor for the benefit."

"Oh, really?"

"Yes, at the last minute some company wanted to donate a bucket of money. They're paying to have the entire lobby renovated next year. Top to bottom."

"That's great," I say, but then I'm interrupted by Mrs. Banner clinking a spoon on her crystal champagne flute. "The awards are about to start, everyone, so let's move on into the North Living Room, shall we?"

Everyone follows her through a hallway past what seems like a never-ending collection of rooms to the other side of the building. The North Living Room could fit a medium-size electronics store inside it. Preston takes me to a seat in the front row near a potted palm. There is enough room for everyone to sit with space to spare, and once everyone has found a seat, the lights dim to a soft glow and the TV pops on.

The opening shows the outside of the theater in London where the awards are always given. Everyone speaks in a hushed whisper, and the room is almost silent as an announcer introduces the show and the screen shows people entering the theater. I love the announcer's British accent, since it sounds like Preston.

"The Fifty-Third Annual Seggerman Awards, featuring the brightest stars in the theater and independent film. The awards this year are brought to you by Tesco Markets, making good things better. Healthy One Meals, don't you deserve a Healthy One? And HappyWow energy drink, it's HappyWow!"

"Ahhh!" I scream. I actually scream like I'm plunging down a roller coaster, and everyone looks over at me. I can't believe it! HappyWow is like some creature in a horror movie showing up when I least expect it. If they're a sponsor, that means there will be a HappyWow commercial during this broadcast. How can this be happening?

"Are you all right?" Preston asks.

The only thing I can think to say is, "Sorry. My toe stub from yesterday is acting up. Um, I think I should use the restroom. Where's the closest one?" Why anyone would need to use the restroom to help a stubbed toe, I don't know.

Preston points me down the hall, but the apartment is so large I can barely follow his instructions. I get up and almost run out of the room. Luckily, everyone has their eyes glued to the TV, so I'm able to escape unnoticed.

I make my way down the hall, through the living room, and remember that I saw a bathroom next to the terrace. I go in and shut the door.

Think, Isabel. Think.

Maybe they won't recognize me. Then I remember the glimpse of the commercial I saw on Gladys's television, and I realize even the doorman would be able to pick me out of a police lineup after seeing the commercial. I am about to be humiliated in front of a room of the most important people in the theater world. I look at myself in the mirror, determined to find a solution. I almost start hyperventilating and consider going out on the terrace for some fresh air, but it's freezing out there. Then it hits me.

The terrace.

I quietly leave the bathroom and make my way to the terrace door. I hope I'm able to beat the first commercial break. As I open the door, a freezing blast of arctic wind blows into the apartment. It's a cold night, and high on the penthouse floor, thirty-three stories above the ground, the cold wind is absolutely bone-chilling, but it doesn't matter because this won't take long. I walk outside and shut the door behind me. I'm so full of adrenaline that I barely feel the cold.

I have to find their satellite dish.

There is not much on the terrace except for the massive trees and bushes, which have been covered in burlap for the winter. I walk all the way around toward the North Living Room. When I finally make it around the corner, I see the black plastic dish receiving the signal that is about to destroy any potential I have for a career.

The problem is the dish is on the other side of the North Living Room, which has three large windows between where I'm standing and where the dish is located. I examine the windows carefully. There's about two feet of wall before the window starts. If I crawl along on the ground for a few yards, I could make it to the dish. It'll be hard to do without ruining my dress, because there's a huge puddle on the terrace from last night's freezing rain. I look around and see the covered plants and suddenly get an idea. I turn to one of the shrubs and rip off the rough burlap covering. I lie down on the fabric and use it as a shield as I shimmy across the floor, leaving my dress unharmed.

This has to work.

As I get closer to the windows, I can hear the guests inside laughing together and gently applauding as the first award is announced. I pass by the first window and then stand up and walk a few yards hidden by the building wall. I repeat this two more times until I'm next to the satellite dish.

I walk over to the dish and examine it. I could just rip the thing off the terrace wall and throw it down to Central Park, but I realize that might leave a lot of questions, and the falling object could seriously hurt someone. Why should the fact that my life is being ruined ruin someone else's?

I spot a small cable that goes from the wall to the edge of the dish. That must be carrying the signal, and even if it's not, it looks important enough to hopefully shut down the whole operation. I don't have a second to waste. I grab both ends and pull hard. Nothing. It won't budge. I gather all my strength and count to three in my head and pull again. This time the two ends disconnect.

Then I hear it. "Oh no," and "What happened?" I can see through the window that the gentle blue light of the telecast has changed to a pulsating gray, which means they are all watching static. Mission accomplished.

I shimmy under the windows again so I can get back to Preston without being missed. I quickly run to the other side of the terrace, where the door I came out of is. I plan to rejoin the party and pretend to be as upset as everyone else that the satellite went out. Before I open the door, I brush off my dress, which looks no worse for wear, and go to open the door.

It's stuck.

I try again and use the same strength I used to disconnect the cable, but it won't budge. One more try—until I realize it's locked. I run to the door on the other side of the terrace. Same thing. There is one more door even farther down on the terrace. I run to it and try to open it. Nothing.

It's freezing. My teeth start chattering. I consider banging on the door and praying that the housekeeper or one of the other staff members will hear me. Suddenly I see one of the servers in a maid's uniform cleaning up. I bang on the door, assuming it's loud enough for her to hear, but she doesn't react at all. I bang again and stare at her, willing her to hear me, but when I look closely I see she has earbuds in her ears.

I rub my arms with my hands to generate some heat and walk back to the door I came out of to see if anyone is around. A few minutes go by and no one shows up. Surely Preston will start wondering what has happened to me.

Then I see one of the guests walk by, wearing his coat and walking to the door. Then another, then a couple, and then a small group of people. Everyone is leaving.

I did it. I actually did it. I'm so happy that I start clapping my hands together, because this not only allows me to express my joy but also warms me up for a few seconds. Then I add some jumping into the mix. As I'm beginning to jump and clap harder, I see Preston walking toward the terrace, but before I can do anything he spots me, comes over, and opens the door.

"What in the world are you doing out there? You'll catch your death of cold," he says, and takes off his blazer and puts it around me.

"My stubbed toe needed some air," I say. At least being out there so long gave me time to think of an excuse, albeit a feeble one.

"Well, the satellite went out. Everyone's going home because we called the TV company, and they don't have any problem on their end so they think something is wrong here. They have no idea if it will even come back."

"That's awful," I say. "I was really looking forward to watching your mom enjoy seeing Norma Swenson cry."

"Well, we can watch it online next week, I guess, and that way we don't have to sit through those bloody awful commercials."

"Preston, that just goes to show you, there's a bright side to everything."

CHAPTER 38

In the lobby of Preston's building, I take out my cell phone to call my dad and let him know I'm going to use the cab money he gave me for an early return. But before I can call him, I see that I missed a text that must have come in when I was in the elevator. It's from Brittany: BUNCH OF US AT AN ARCADE IN TIMES SQUARE YOU MUST COME MEET US! IMPORTANT! 911!

As I'm reading the first text another one comes in: MEET US NOW. YOU WILL NOT BELIEVE THIS.

I have no idea what she's talking about, but I figure it's still very early, and Times Square is on the way home, so I decide to make a quick stop to find out what's going on. I text back: ON MY WAY.

The doorman helps me hail a cab, and I direct the driver to take me to the corner where the arcade is located in Times Square. The cab rushes down the street, and Central Park flashes by on one side while elegant skyscrapers flash by on the other. I lean back in my seat and think about what I just did. I had such high expectations for this evening. Preston did call it a date when he asked me. I guess if I hadn't destroyed the satellite signal, the night might have ended differently. Maybe he would have kissed me good-bye on the cheek, and maybe this time his lips would have been closer to my cheek than my ear. But once the satellite broke down, everyone sort of filed out of the apartment, and there was no chance for Preston to give me a proper good-bye. On the other hand, I guess if he really wanted to, he would have found a way. Right?

"This good, miss?" the cabdriver says, and I look out the window and see Brittany with Cassie, Phoebe, Liam, and Chuck. What's Chuck doing here? Of course, he's friends with all of them. Why wouldn't he be here?

I was pretty rude to Chuck the last time I saw him, and I regret it now. Why couldn't I keep my big mouth shut about *Ninja Lunchroom*? I wonder if he knows I went with Brittany and her family to see *Super Claw*—and more importantly, I wonder if he knows I brought Preston.

I pay the cabdriver as Brittany rushes over to open my door. "Well, here she is, everybody," she says. "The top banana."

She says the last part in a weird sort of way, and I don't really know what she means, but for some reason it makes everybody laugh. Except Chuck. He smiles and looks at me.

"Hey, Isabel. How you doing?" he asks.

"What's going on? What's the big emergency?"

"Well . . ." Chuck begins, but before he can finish, Brittany steps in.

"No, I'll show her." Brit grabs my hand and guides me down the sidewalk. "Now close your eyes," she says, and I close them immediately. Brittany is not the kind of girl you disobey.

"Well, we were all hanging out and playing some video games after going to the amusement park. When we came out of the arcade . . ." She slows down and turns me around carefully. Then she gently puts her hand on my chin and tilts my head up. "We saw this. Open your eyes!"

"Ahhh!" I scream. I blink and then again, "Ahhh!" It's the same toe-stubbing scream I've been using for the past few days, but since I'm in the middle of Times Square, I don't have to hold back and no one cares. I scream again with abandon. "Ahhh!"

"I know," Brittany says. "You're so lucky. I had no idea this campaign was going to be so big. I should have locked you in that broom closet when I had the chance." Everyone looks a little nervous, because they all know Brittany isn't kidding.

Times Square is chaos. There are theater marquees, outdoor cafés, tourists, street performers, and just regular New Yorkers. Above all this chaos is the one thing that trumps everything: the mega Jumbotron, which is more than four stories tall and about half a block wide. There are some counties in some states that I'm sure are smaller than this screen. I stare at it with a mixture of shock, terror, and just plain exhaustion.

My face is the size of a building!

My Jumbotron self is hopping and dancing around like someone put spiders in my shoes. Granted, most of my body has been replaced by a computer-generated animated banana, but those are *my* arms and *my* legs, and anyone who has ever met me for more than a second would be able to tell that's *my face*, whether it's the size of a soccer field or not.

"This . . . is . . . awful," I say.

"I think the spot is really cute," Cassie says. "I saw it a couple times yesterday while I was watching *American Star*. I love the part where you slide down the rainbow into the blender. It's so funny."

"And the animation is really cool. I love the colors they used. It almost looks like manga," Liam says.

They're trying to make me feel better, but it doesn't work.

"I thought you didn't want this to be such a big deal," Chuck says while everyone else is staring up at the screen and pointing.

"I didn't," I tell him.

"And you know, these guys are happy for you. I mean really happy for you. They can't stop talking about it, so I don't think they're making fun of you or anything. They think you're totally cool. And so do I."

I should say something. I should say what I feel. I should tell him that I'm humiliated and scared and confused about . . . everything. For once in my life I should go with my gut and not my head, but I can't, and anyway it's too late.

Everyone except Chuck has moved a few yards

away from the curb to get a better look at the Jumbotron and take pictures with their cell phones. Everyone is fascinated with Banana Isabel except Chuck, who is still right next to me looking at Real Isabel, right into my eyes. I can't handle it. It's all too much. I decide to make my getaway.

"Tell everybody thanks for the texts and telling me about it and everything, but I think I really need to go," I say. I run to the other side of the block to hail a cab without even saying good-bye. I just want to be alone.

CHAPTER 39

Luckily, the day of the benefit I spend most of my time underground. Literally. The dressing rooms for the theater are in the basement. This means there is no cell or wireless service, so I'm pretty much cut off from the rest of the world, and I'm grateful.

My dressing room is all the way at the end of the hall, and it's my sanctuary for the day. We started the morning going through the lighting cues, so even though I spent some time with Preston onstage, we really didn't get a chance to interact that much. I could, however, tell that HappyWow hasn't yet made its way to the Banner household, since Preston doesn't wince when he looks at me.

I spend most of the day avoiding him, telling him I need to get into character and go over my lines. Really, I'm in my dressing room. Hiding.

About fifteen minutes before the curtain, I

sneak out of my dressing room in the long pink-and-plum brocade gown I'm wearing to play Juliet and go to peek through a hole in the curtain to see who might be in the audience. It's very unprofessional, I know, but at this point, my career is a train wreck waiting to happen, so what have I got to lose? I go to the main stage and easily find a small enough hole that will allow me to see without being seen. I scan the audience, and it takes me only a few moments to spot the most important movers and shakers in the theater world. Besides award-winning actors, I see producers I recognize from prominent theater companies and a few directors who I have auditioned for in the past. And there . . . in the middle of the theater is . . . no. It can't be . . . it's not possible. I'm just imagining it.

I step away from the curtain to catch my breath. Could they be here? I go to look through the hole again to make sure it's just my imagination playing tricks on me, but before I can, the stage manager comes by and says, "We need the stage clear. We have to test the video for the final presentation."

"Of course," I say. I quickly walk away from the curtain and into the wings. I walk down the hallway and open the door to my dressing room. When I see what's sitting at my makeup mirror, I let out a little yelp and quickly close the door so no one sees.

"Chernique!" I yell. The dressing rooms in the basement have pretty thick walls, so I don't need to hold back.

"Well, at least you didn't slam the door on me. This is definitely an improvement."

"The benefit is about to begin. You know you're supposed to be in your seat and *not* backstage."

"Well, it's not my fault. You don't have any cell phone reception, and I needed to talk to you. Anyway, I told everyone that I'd be back at my seat before the show started."

"Everyone?" I ask. "Aren't you here with just your mom and my parents?"

"Yeah, but Brittany and all your commercial friends are here. Brittany's dad bought, like, a whole row of seats or something." I look at the clock on the wall and realize there are only ten minutes until curtain time.

"Um, Isabel, do you remember that summer when you went to visit your aunt and you asked me to take care of your goldfish, Marlin Brando?"

"You came backstage to remind me about the goldfish you killed?"

"Not exactly. But remember how we got into that fight because I just came out and told you, 'Marlin Brando is dead?' You told me I should have told you gradually in order to prepare you. One day I should have said, 'Marlin's not eating.' Then the next day, 'Marlin is looking tired.' And so on."

"Yes," I say slowly, wondering where all this is leading.

"Well, I've got news. Marlin Brando is dead."

"What?" I ask. I have no idea what she's talking about.

"Look, there's no easy way to tell you this, so I'm just gonna say it. When I got to my seat, I was looking through the program, and HappyWow is the new sponsor of the benefit." Chernique hands the program to me like a trapped gunman handing over his pistol. I open it to the listing of events for the evening.

I scan down the list and see that the final event after our scene from *Romeo and Juliet* is a "HappyWow Presentation."

The commercial must be the video the stage-hand was talking about upstairs. Now it all makes sense. I wasn't hallucinating. It was them. That was Mr. Fukishima and Miko in the audience.

"Chernique!!" I scream. "Do you realize how bad this is? How awful? How monumentally terrible? We are talking beyond epic here. The most important people in theater are here." I grab Chernique by the shoulder and begin shaking her. "Mrs. Banner is here. Preston IS HERE! I can't just disconnect a satellite this time."

Chernique pulls herself out of my grip and says, "So what? You have enough money to pay for school with the commercial you booked." She stretches her shoulders and adds, "And don't *ever* shake my shoulders like that again. It hurts."

"Chernique," I say, ignoring her request for the time being, "I need that scholarship. I talked to Honey. I'll have a lot of money, but I'll still need that scholarship if I ever want to graduate. What am I gonna do?"

The loudspeaker in the dressing room crackles. "We are at five minutes until places. Five minutes until places."

"Look, you better get back to your seat," I say. I'm not angry. I'm not in a panic. I'm numb.

"I can't leave you like this," Chernique says.

"Just meet me after. I need time to myself to prepare." I take a deep breath in and let it out.

"I only wanted to warn you," she says.

"I know. You're a good a friend," I say.

"You are too," she says, and goes to open the door. But before she reaches the knob, she turns back to me and says, "And you're one heck of an actor!" She opens the door and leaves.

There's only one thing I can do, and it's the only thing I really know how to do. If I'm going to be humiliated after my scene, I'm going to make sure I give the best performance of my entire life.

CHAPTER 40

And I do.

At the end of our scene, the audience erupts in applause. Performing Juliet was one of the greatest theatrical challenges of my life, and I'm proud of the work I did onstage. Preston and I smile at each other, and while his smile shows gratitude and relief, mine still displays some anxiety, because I know the audience will get to see one more sample of my performing abilities before the night is through. We bow slowly, and the audience continues to clap. Preston squeezes my hand and I smile. This time I'm only thinking about him and our fine work on the stage. We bow a second and third time but leave while the audience is still clapping.

As soon as we're offstage, the lights change and the screen descends from the rafters. It might as well be a hangman's noose. A stagehand places a podium on the stage, and Mr. Tipton enters. The audience applauds politely, and Mr. Tipton moves his hands in front of his body in a gesture that gently asks the audience to stop.

"Please, please hold your applause. I am but a humble servant to the artists you have seen tonight. Let's give another round of applause to all these artists who so generously donated their time, talent, and energy toward making tonight a success."

The audience applauds again. "Speaking of tonight's success, I am here to welcome a new donor to our organization. Their generosity will not only keep the lights on for a few years but also allow us to build a new rehearsal space and completely renovate the lobby."

The audience applauds again, and I tug on Preston's sleeve. I can't bear the thought of him laughing *at* me in the commercial. I decide I have to tell him about it before he actually sees it. Mrs. Banner invited me to join Preston and a bunch of people at Sardi's after the benefit. My plan was to explain everything to him then. I would sit him down and explain how I never thought the commercial would air in this country, let alone at the end of the benefit. We'd find a nice quiet corner of the restaurant, and

I would tell him everything. But with only seconds until impact, I realize I have to tell him *now*. I have to. It will give me some small bit of control in a situation that is completely spinning out of control. "I need to speak to you," I say.

"Don't you want to hear Mr. Tipton's speech?"

"Yes," I say, "but I need to speak to you." He follows me to an area next to the stage but behind the wings. "Preston . . . I wanted to tell you . . ." I can't seem to find the words.

"Quick, we don't want to miss the big screening. What do you want to tell me?"

We can hear Mr. Tipton from the stage. "This wonderful drink is made with many different fruits and vitamins, but most importantly it's made with bananas."

"That's me!" I finally say, and point toward Mr. Tipton.

"Who? You're Mr. Tipton?"

"The world's best and most delicious banana in the world!" Mr. Tipton says loudly.

I repeat, "That's me. THAT'S ME. I'M THAT BANANA!"

Before Preston can respond, the lights go dim, and I hear *"Tang. Tang. Clang. Clang."* And from the wings I see the lights on the screen flicker and my alter ego, the HappyWow banana, appears. At first, Preston just watches.

I can hear the audience laughing. Minutes ago I was doing a dramatic scene and had them in the palm of my hand, ready to feel my every emotion. I was dying for the love of my life and had the audience feeling the utter hopelessness of Juliet's fate. Now it's my own real hopelessness onstage as the banana that is me slides down the rainbow into the blender and everyone laughs. It might as well be all my hopes and dreams going into that blender.

"Isabel, is that . . ." He pauses and looks at the screen and then at me. "Is that *you*?"

I just nod my head and give a sort of half smile. I try to look girly and cute in my Juliet costume. Girly and cute is not really my thing, but hey, at this point I'll try anything.

"You are a jumping banana!" he says, and even his sweet British accent with its emphasis on the second syllable can't hide the fact that he is both shocked and disgusted.

"Well, technically, no," I say. "If you look closely, I'm only bouncing on one foot in the take they used, so I'm not really jumping. I'm hopping."

"Isabel!" he says. His voice is full of disappointment. "How could you?"

"I can explain everything. Let's change out of our costumes and go and meet your mother at Sardi's. Okay?"

He looks at me. He doesn't say anything. Even though the silence is only a few seconds, it's suffocating.

"Let's go to Sardi's and talk," I plead.

Finally he speaks. "Sardi's? Isabel, really? Do you think my mother is going to want to be at Sardi's with a dancing banana? I think by now you know that my family has a certain reputation and image to uphold. The Banners have standards."

I straighten my spine slightly and bristle a bit at the implied accusation that I don't have standards. I try to remain calm and speak gently. "Why don't we just talk?"

He looks me up and down and says, "I don't think so." Then he turns and walks away.

How. Dare. He. How *dare* he not give me a chance to explain? It's one thing to make a decision to drop me, but it's another thing to do it without even having a conversation with me. Without hearing my side of the story. How dare he!

The sight of Preston's backside makes me want to walk up to it and kick it with my foot. Hard! What a creep he is. What a self-important little stuck-up brat. I want to shout at him and tell him off, but it takes only a second to realize that a boy like Preston isn't worth my time. The least, the very least, he could have done was talk to me. Chernique and my parents and all my new commercial friends understood why I was doing it. Why can't he? Truth is, he didn't care enough to stick around and find out. I should have listened to Chernique when she told me he was a snob. I can't believe I'll have to see him in the halls at school next year.

Then it hits me.

I'm not going to have to worry about seeing him in the halls at school next year, because there is *no way* they're going to let me keep the Banner scholarship. The money from the commercial is not going to be enough to cover all the costs until I graduate. Everything I worked so hard for over the past months is gone. It's floated up to the sky and evaporated just like that. It's over.

"There she is!" Mr. Tipton's voice booms. I look over to find him walking toward me. I guess I'm about to get dumped again, but when I look closely at Mr. Tipton, I see he is smiling as he approaches me. What could he be thinking?

CHAPTER 41

Before Mr. Tipton says another word, I jump in with a desperate attempt to manage the situation. "Look, Mr. Tipton, I really can explain this whole thing. I know you're terribly disappointed in me, but—"

"Disappointed? In you? Are you out of your mind, young lady? How in the world could I be disappointed in you? First, you give the finest performance of Shakespeare I have seen in my life." He puts his hand to his mouth like he's telling me something that should not be overheard. "And don't tell anyone, but I've had a *very* long life. Second, I get to show off to everyone your comedic talent and skill at physical comedy."

"But everyone was laughing at me," I say.

"Everyone was laughing. Period. They were laughing because your performance is so good. Your talent is what was making them laugh. You're hysterical and you don't even know it. I can't think of anyone like you who is equal parts Meryl Streep and Lucille Ball. I'm thrilled to have you at the academy next year."

"You mean, you aren't kicking me out?"

"Now why would I kick out our most talented student?" he asks. I can't believe Mr. Tipton, *the* Mr. Tipton, is being so understanding and giving me the hugest compliment of my career. This was not the reaction I was expecting.

"Thank you," I tell him. "But the scholarship? I can't attend without it, and Mrs. Banner . . ." I trail off. We both know Mrs. Banner will never allow me to darken her good name.

"Don't you worry about her. It may be *her* scholarship, but it's *my* school. You didn't do anything wrong. I'm sure Patricia will see it otherwise, but you were using your talents to make a living. It's not the same thing as exploiting yourself on some reality show. Not at all. I'll have a little chat with Peppy the Peanut Butter Elf."

"Excuse me?" I say.

"Well, you won't find this on Wikipedia or anywhere else, for that matter, but before Patricia Banner was *Patricia Banner,* she was widely recognized across the UK as Peppy the Peanut Butter Elf. The Banner name may come with a great deal of prestige, but it did not come with a lot of money. Patricia had to work hard to earn everything she has, and sometimes she forgets that. How do you think we met?"

"During the Broadway production of *Cat on a Hot Tin Roof*. You both won Tonys," I say plainly.

"We knew each other well before that. I directed the very first Peppy the Peanut Butter Elf commercial. I was the one who cast Patricia as Peppy. I don't think she'll give you any problems, or the old videotapes I have of those commercials might just find their way to the Internet."

"Oh, thank you, Mr. Tipton."

"It is I who should be thanking you for the beautiful performance and for the beautiful artist I know you will become."

CHAPTER 42

I change out of my Juliet costume quickly. I'm sure Preston is already on his way to Sardi's, but I don't even care if we cross paths. I'd much rather be eating ice cream sundaes at the Lafayette with the people who know me and accept me for who I am than dining on some icy sorbet with a lot of phonies I don't even know.

I walk out of my dressing room and up the stairs. The crew is already taking down the set and getting ready for the next production. It reminds me of another reason I love the theater. As soon as one production ends, another one starts. I turn the corner to get to the stage door and run smack into Chuck.

"What are you doing backstage?" I ask. The way I keep smacking into him, I think he's pretty brave to be within fifty feet of me.

"Um, Chernique," he says. "She told me I had to go backstage to see if she left her sunglasses here." His voice warbles a bit as he speaks. I can't tell if he's nervous or onto the fact that Chernique must have been making something up to get him backstage with me. "I tried to tell her that it's night and she wasn't wearing sunglasses, but she's very hard to say no to."

"You've noticed?"

"Yeah," he says, and nods his head. His thick dark hair falls gently across the top of his forehead. Then he pulls a beautiful bouquet of violets out from behind his back. "These are for you. I heard you like violets."

"Wow, thank you," I say, and gently take them from him. I look down at the deep purple petals and green leaves. They are such a dramatic color yet have such a simple form. I've gotten flowers after a performance many times before, but they've never made me feel the way these particular ones do. For the first time I really understand why boys give girls flowers. They make me feel beautiful and fragile at the same time.

"You were fantastic tonight. In everything. I mean it. You made me want to go back and read

Twelfth Night. That's my favorite. I mean my favorite comedy. *Hamlet* is my overall favorite Shakespeare play."

"Mine too," I say. "You like Shakespeare? I thought you liked action movies and special effects."

"Can't a person like both?"

I think about his question for a second. I guess I thought people liked one thing or the other. Either you liked impressionist painting *or* paintball games. Filet mignon or cheeseburgers. But it doesn't have to be one or the other. You can like both. Why not? You can appear onstage in a dramatic play and on TV in a comedic commercial. It seems so simple, but figuring this out for the first time really overwhelms me. You can like both. You can *be* both.

And I have the perfect example of this right in front of me. Chuck likes both, and I think he might even like both Isabels. I was so caught up in Preston and the Banner name that I couldn't see what a great boy I had right in front of me this whole time.

I finally answer his question. "Yes, I suppose you can like both."

"That's cool," he says. "We should go see a production of *Hamlet* the next time it's playing."

"Sounds good," I say. "But I have a better idea."

"Oh yeah? What?"

"How about we go see an IMAX screening of *Ninja Lunchroom*?"

"*Nina Lunchroom*?" he asks. A wide smile appears across his face, and his dark, piercing eyes dance a bit.

"As long as you don't mind seeing it a second time," I say.

"Well actually, it would be my fourth," he says, and we both laugh. "I thought you hated movies like that."

"Let's just say, I think I'm beginning to understand their appeal." With that we head out the stage door to find everyone else. Chernique, Brittany, Liam, Phoebe, and Cassie are all waiting for me. They each congratulate me on my performance, and we have one massive group hug.

CHAPTER 43

"*And the Seggerman Award for Best Supporting* Actress in a Dramatic Film goes to . . ." The handsome young actor in a crisp formal tuxedo fumbles with an envelope before announcing, "Norma Swenson."

Everyone applauds. Somewhere in the world I know Mrs. Banner is gritting her teeth. I applaud enthusiastically, since I'm not entirely sure if the cameras are still beaming my face along with the other nominees' faces across the world or if they have cut to Norma onstage accepting the small gold statue of a figure holding a theatrical mask. Norma's performance was remarkable, and she has been nominated almost half a dozen times, so I knew my chances of winning were very slim. I know it's a cliché to say that it's an honor just to be nominated, but it's true. When my agent, Lenny, called to say that my performance in the film *Yesterday's Answer* was nominated, I started jumping up and down. Once I was able to regain my composure, the first thing I did was call Mr. Fukishima.

"Thank you, Hiro. Thank you so much for everything," I told him. At that point we were on a first-name basis, and I knew that his English was much better than he let on.

It's hard to believe that when I booked the commercial for HappyWow just over a year ago, it would lead to getting nominated for a Seggerman Award. Of course, at the time I was so concerned with what people would think of me being a happy yet proud dancing banana that I didn't take the time to even look up Hiro Fukishima on IMDB. If I had, I would have found out that he was not only the creator of the new energy drink but also an award-winning director in Japan, whose films are recognized at the world's most prestigious film festivals, like Cannes and Sundance.

When Hiro asked me to be in his new independent feature film, I learned all about his important film projects. I think the fact that people have more than one side to them has finally sunk in. You can direct commercials *and* great works of art. You can make people laugh as a dancing banana and you can make them cry as a runaway with a secret. Being an artist is not about being any one thing. In fact, it's not about being at all. It's about seeing and feeling, and I think I'm finally starting to understand that.

Preston, on the other hand, seems to see the same old things. The day my nomination was announced, he had an arrangement of red and white roses sent to me with a card congratulating me and asking me to call him. The roses looked like they were manufactured in some flower laboratory, and the sentiment on the card seemed equally as genuine—which is to say, not at all. I threw out the card, brought the roses to a senior center, and never called him.

The presenters begin to read the nominees for the next category, and the cameraman, who was positioned in front of me, capturing my face in a close-up, moves on to the next nominee. I feel my phone vibrate through the side of my tiny black sequined purse. I discreetly take it out and look at the screen. It says: YOU WERE ROBBED!

Under the text is a picture of all my friends waving. Since I could only take my parents with me, they all gathered at Brittany's place to watch the awards via satellite. Luckily, karma did not rear its vengeful head and destroy the signal. In the picture Chernique is smiling in the center. Chuck is next to her and has his hands in the shape of a heart. Cassie and Phoebe are smiling their best commercial smiles, and Liam and Brittany are holding up pictures they drew of me holding my very own award. I text back: MISS U ALL! THANKS!

My dad leans over to me and whispers, "They're right. You were robbed."

It's funny—I don't feel that way at all. I sit back in my plush seat, and as the rest of the awards are handed out, I feel like the luckiest girl in the world.

ABOUT THE AUTHOR

P. G. Kain has been on hundreds and hundreds of commercial auditions for everything from a talking taco to a mad cupcake scientist. He has even booked a few spots. He is on faculty at New York University, where he is the chair of Contemporary Culture and Creative Production in Global Liberal Studies. As a Faculty Fellow in Residence at NYU, P. G. lives among nine hundred undergraduate students in a residence hall near Gramercy Park. You can reach P. G. and get commercial tips at www.TweenInk.com.

Sometimes a girl just needs a good book.
Lauren Barnholdt understands.

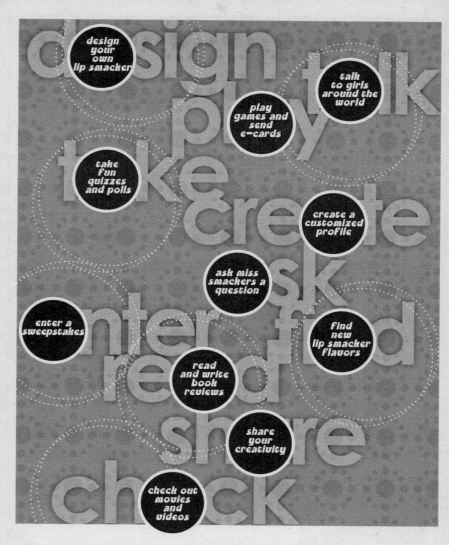

Jammed full of surprises!

LiP SMACKER.
LOUNGE

VISIT US AT WWW.LIPSMACKERLOUNGE.COM!